STARTING FROM SCRATCH

CHRISTINE GAEL

FROG PRINTS PUBLISHING LLC

INTRODUCTION

A story of love, sisterhood, and starting over...

Lena Merrill and Owen McEnna have been best friends for decades, and she's done a great job of pretending she's not in love with him that whole time...until recently. Maybe it's all the changes in the air. Maybe it's realizing that life is passing her by and most of her dreams are still unfulfilled. Whatever the case, her already notoriously bad poker face is slipping, and it needs to stop, pronto. Because there's only one thing worse than not having Owen love her back, and that's the thought of driving him away altogether.

When Nikki Merrill set off to find her long lost sister, Anna, she never imagined she'd be returning home to Cherry Blossom Point with her in tow. Battle lines are drawn when each of her siblings have wildly different reactions to their new family member. Lena is willing to invite Anna into their lives, Gayle and Jack can't even look at her, and Nikki? She's caught dead in the middle of things. Will building a relationship with her new sister splinter the one she has with the siblings she's always known?

Anna Sullivan didn't want another family. Now that she has one, though, she's in for the long haul. When she leaves Bluebird Bay to spend some time with Nikki and meet the rest of her siblings, she isn't prepared for the drama that ensues. It's kind of hard to make a good impression when half of them see her as a walking representation of their father's infidelity. And when more family secrets are uncovered, she realizes they've only seen the tip of the iceberg.

Will Anna figure out how to navigate these choppy family waters, or will her visit to Cherry Blossom Point turn out to be a disaster of Titanic proportions?

1

NIKKI

Nikki Merrill stood in her kitchen, surveying the breakfast she was making for her sister, Anna. The waffles were almost done, the fruit was all cut, the hollandaise was finished... she just needed to poach the eggs, but that could wait until the last minute.

Might as well make a fruit compote for the waffles, she decided, pulling a bag of frozen berries from the freezer.

Okay, so maybe cooking entirely too much food for one meal was a nervous habit. But it was soothing.

She sniffed the air, rife with the scent of melted butter and maple syrup warming, and let out a sigh. God, it felt good to be in her home again after being away for so long. It had surprised her...the sense of comfort she'd felt when she'd walked in. She hadn't been at all homesick during her stay in Bluebird Bay. Sure, she had missed her daughter, but Beth was away at college anyway. And the time away from her family here had actually given her some much-needed clarity. No, she hadn't missed all that much about Cherry Blossom Point...except her kitchen.

She had to admit, it was a chef's dream. Literally. Nikki had scrimped and saved for years as she'd planned every detail of the kitchen she'd wanted her whole life. The rest of the house was a hodgepodge of generic box-store furniture and household bric-a-brac that had been left on the side of the road with a *Free* sign. The walls were bare of art, save for a few childhood photos of Beth, and the rugs were nearly worn through. It didn't usually bother her, but she had almost been embarrassed showing Anna around when they'd arrived two nights before. The dusty living room with its one yellow couch and one gray. The outdated bathroom with its pale pink tiles. Beth's bedroom, where Anna currently slept, still a garish shade of purple that Beth had chosen six years ago at the age of thirteen.

The kitchen, though?

The kitchen was the bomb, and Nikki's sanctuary. Each item had been chosen with the utmost care, and she had done most of the renovations herself. She had tiled the floor—twice, when her first efforts had been lackluster—painted the cabinets a pale dove gray, and installed each handle and knob herself. The Blue Damasco marble countertops were a work of art, and the collection of copper pots and pans hanging on the wall never failed to lift Nikki's spirits. It had taken her five years to save up for her Lacanche range, and she loved that thing like a second child. Sure, she'd taken her chef's knives and a few other essentials with her to Bluebird Bay, but lord... she had missed this kitchen.

She lifted the handle on the waffle maker, noting the pale golden color of the waffles, before closing it again. Two more minutes, tops.

She hadn't had access to this outlet in months. Rented

apartment kitchenettes and slinging hash at Mo's Diner just didn't have the same feel as cooking food in her own home. And if she made enough for an army? Well, it never hurt to have some extra waffles in the freezer, just in case. Back when Beth was younger, Nikki used to make a huge batch of waffles every Sunday and just pop them into the toaster oven on weekday mornings for a quick breakfast. All the convenience of a toaster waffle, but a hundred times better.

"Coffee?" Anna asked blearily as she shuffled in.

"There." Nikki pointed past the gently steaming waffle maker to the fresh pot of coffee in the corner.

Anna poured herself a cup and went to sit at the table, scrolling through her phone while she rejoined the land of the living.

Nikki hoped that her sister hadn't been sleeping too poorly on the lumpy mattress in Beth's room... if Nikki had known that her sister was going to come stay with her, she would have been better prepared.

She watched her sister from under her lashes, noting the hazel eyes so like her own. Who would've thought just a couple months ago that Anna would be here right now? Nikki had gone to Bluebird Bay in hopes of meeting her father Eric's other daughter, who had been the product of an affair he'd had while already married to Nikki's mother. It hadn't been an easy decision to go. Her much-older brother, Jack, and his twin, Gayle, had nearly lost their minds.

"Let sleeping dogs lie, Nikki. Why bring more attention to Dad's terrible betrayal?"

Her sister Lena had been more diplomatic.

"If you need to go do it to feel settled, do it. I'm here for you."

And her father? Despite keeping the secret from them until after their mother passed out of respect for her feelings, he'd been all for it. In fact, he'd had hopes that maybe, if Nikki broke the ice and was able to actually connect with Anna in a meaningful way, he might get to meet her someday too. She hadn't been as optimistic as all that, and knew it was a risk to even try. Anna was a fifty-year-old woman with a life of her own. One she might not want disrupted by some stranger barging in on account of them sharing some of the same DNA.

Nikki had been dead right on that count. Initially, Anna had slammed the door shut on any attempts to get to know her. But she had stuck it out for weeks, hoping...waiting. She'd all but given up when Anna had finally relented and agreed to see her. Nikki had been sure it would be a one-time thing. When it had blossomed into more, she'd been ecstatic. They might live two hours apart, but by the time she'd packed up and was ready to leave Bluebird Bay, she knew she would see her sister again. Given their rocky start, she'd been satisfied with that.

So, two days ago, when Anna had told Nikki that she was going with her to Cherry Blossom Point?

Nikki was floored.

"Are you serious?" she'd asked.

"As a heart attack," Anna had replied. *"You're my sister, Nikki, and you've felt like my sister from the moment I finally let my guard down. And Beth already feels as dear to me as the nieces I've known their whole lives. You saw how she fit in on Thanksgiving. It was like the both of you had always been there. I can't imagine not having you guys in my life. I can't believe I almost missed out on that, just by being pig-*

headed. I want to meet my biological father. There are so many things I wish I'd said to Pop before he passed away. Things that I should have done with my mom before she got too sick to do them, adventures we could have had together...I'm too old to keep making the same mistakes, Nikki. I don't want to miss my chance to get to know our dad. I don't want to live with one more regret over what I should *have done. Family comes first, and if something happened and I never got to meet him? I think it would feel like another loss, in some ways."*

As soon as Nikki had caught her breath, she'd agreed without really thinking it through. More time to get to know her funny, whip-smart, sassy older sister, who was brave in ways that Nikki could only dream of. But on the two-hour drive to Cherry Blossom Point, doubts had begun to creep in. As they began to pass familiar buildings—and the street that their brother Jack lived on—she'd started to freak out a little.

Internally, at least.

Outwardly, she had tried to keep calm... but she was never much of a pretender.

She swallowed a sigh and cracked an egg into the swirling vinegar water. They'd been here two days and she still had no clue how to handle this part of things. Who should she tell first? Initially, she'd considered calling a family meeting. Letting them all know at once. Just rip off the band-aid in one fell swoop. Was that a terrible idea?

She'd had a nightmare about it the night before—Gayle had given her a look of withering disappointment, Jack had loomed over them all and lectured them until Nikki had started to cry, and Anna had started disintegrating, blowing away like dust.

She bit back a groan and scooped the perfectly poached egg from the water and transferred it to a paper towel.

Maybe she would call Lena first or go straight to Dad. After all, he was the one Anna had come to meet, and she was well aware that Jack and Gayle wanted nothing more than to sweep this part of their family history under the rug and had no interest in meeting her. But despite the whopper he'd managed to keep under wraps for decades, Eric Merrill had grown notorious for his inability to keep a secret in his old age. Once he knew, Jack and Gayle wouldn't be far behind.

How would he react to the daughter he had never known? With joy, Nikki hoped. And gratitude. When he'd told them about her, he'd been emotional and clearly indicated that he'd love to meet her. But would the reality of it be too much for him? And could Anna ever truly forgive him for just handing her over and walking away?

It had been a condition imposed by both parties. Nikki's mother had agreed to take Eric back if he never saw Rose or their baby again, and Anna's father had promised Rose that he would raise the baby as his own if she severed all contact with Eric.

What a mess.

But Anna was here now. That was the important thing.

Now she just needed to figure out how to break the news. Her family was expecting her back any day, and their texts and voice messages trying to nail down when that might be were getting more insistent.

Her relationship with Anna was still so new. What if her siblings acted like jerks? Nikki trusted Lena to be kind, but the twins... What if they treated Anna so poorly that she up and left? What if she wanted nothing to do with *any* of them anymore?

Anna, disintegrating until she disappeared from her life altogether.

No way, Nikki assured herself as she plated their food. She and Beth were part of Anna's family now, for better or for worse. And it was Nikki's job to let her siblings know it. Their dad only lived a few blocks away, and Cherry Blossom Point was a pretty small town. She would hate for them to hear her news from anyone else, and she was running out of time.

It had to be today.

"Breakfast," Nikki announced grimly as she approached the table.

"I'm not sure why you sound like you're about to serve me a severed head," Anna said, setting down her phone, "but that smells amazing. You'd better stop cooking like this; I might never leave. Those meatballs you made last night were a revelation. I can't believe you made pasta from scratch."

Nikki managed a smile. "It's good to be back in my own kitchen."

"Oh wow," Anna said with her mouth full. "This sauce is to die for. Like silk."

"It came out good," Nikki agreed, and for a moment they enjoyed their food in silence.

"So," Anna said, still chewing. "What's the sitch, sis? You ready to bite the bullet yet?"

Nikki gulped and stared at her sister, feeling like a deer caught in the headlights of an oncoming car.

Anna cocked an eyebrow. "Or are we hunkering down here for the foreseeable future? It's fine, either way. I'm just trying to decide if I need to take up knitting. Maybe order Rosetta Stone and brush up on my Italian..."

"I'm not sure what you mean," she stammered, trying to get her head together and think of how to respond. Anna was all-too perceptive. Nikki should've known she couldn't put one past her.

"You're hiding me away like I'm your side chick and your wife is on a business trip."

"Ouch!" Nikki laughed and winced at the same time. "I am not!"

"It's okay, I'm not mad. But let's talk about it," Anna replied, setting her fork down and leaning back in the chair.

"Was it that obvious?" It was amazing how well her sister knew her already.

"Aside from driving to the next town over for groceries at ten PM? Or staying inside all day yesterday to 'settle in'? Or the phone calls and texts you keep ignoring?" Anna shook her head solemnly. "Not obvious at all."

Nikki chuckled and held up a hand. "Okay, okay, I get it."

"What are you afraid of?" Anna asked. "Jack's disapproval? Gayle's anger? Upending everyone's lives? Worst case scenario here is what? Lay it on me."

Nikki pushed some food around on her plate, unable to meet Anna's gaze. "Worst case scenario is that Jack is such a complete ass that you run off and I never see you again."

"Not gonna happen," Anna responded immediately. "Next?"

Nikki looked up as a heavy layer of fear slipped away.

"I'm not here to cause trouble for him...or anyone else," Anna told her. "I just want a little time with Eric, if he'll have me. If anyone else decides they want to meet me, fine. I'm not going to force myself on them."

"Dad will be thrilled. And Lena wants to meet you. She won't say it to the twins, but I'm sure of it." Nikki almost stopped there, for fear of scaring her off, but she deserved to know what she was getting herself into.

"I just don't know about Jack and Gayle," she continued. "Jack is... difficult. He means well. I think. But he's so overbearing. Thinks he's always right, you know? There's never much room for compromise, no gray areas. And he's super bossy. To him, this secret should have stayed buried, and Gayle agreed. They said no good would come of it."

"I don't care about Jack *or* Gayle," Anna said with a shrug. "No skin off my back. I don't have any feelings toward them at all... aside from some irritation that they're stressing out my little sister." She leaned in and took a sip of coffee. "I say we get the truth out there and let the chips fall where they may," she told Nikki. "I deserve the chance to meet my dad if he wants to meet me. And if that's all that happens while I'm here, I'll consider it good." She shrugged. "I'm grateful just to have gotten the bonus sibling, to be honest."

"I'm grateful too. I just hope that Jack and Gayle don't make our lives hell."

"You're really selling the Merrill family dynamic in a big way," Anna quipped, withdrawing her hand and taking a huge bite of her waffles. "Seems like a party in a box."

"Sorry," Nikki said with a chuckle. "They're not all bad. They're just... protective."

"It's not like you live with them, Nikki. You can take space if they try to bully you."

Nikki pushed her plate aside and set her forehead on the

table with a groan. "You haven't met Jack..." she muttered into her placemat.

"The way you're talking, I don't much want to," Anna said lightly. "Let him stay away if he disapproves so much. It's just as well. That way, I only have to juggle one long-lost relative at a time."

The words were barely out of her mouth when the front door swung open and banged against the wall, caught up by the howling November winds. A bundled-up figure tumbled inside. Nikki jumped up from her chair, heart pounding.

"You're home!" Teal green eyes shone bright in a face reddened by cold. Then again, Lena was nearly always pink-cheeked, whether that was from chilly weather or summer sun or simple excitement. Her curly blonde hair was a frizzled mess this morning, sticking out every which way from between her hat and scarf.

"I'm home," Nikki echoed shrilly, panic taking hold as her brain went offline.

Code red. Code red.

Dimly, she heard her sister Lena continue as she closed the door behind her and yanked off her cap.

"Your phone kept going to voicemail, so I wasn't sure if you had stayed longer in Bluebird Bay or if you'd taken a det — Oh, hi!" Lena said brightly. "I didn't realize Nikki had company."

Nikki watched in silent horror as Lena made a beeline toward Anna and then stopped short. Her head whipped toward Nikki, then to Anna, and back again.

The ever-present color leached from her face as she swayed on her feet.

"Holy cannoli."

2

ANNA

ANNA LOOKED between her two sisters, struck dumb.

"I was going to tell you," Nikki was saying to Lena. She looked like she might cry.

Lena remained silent, staring at Anna like she'd just been hit between the eyes with a two-by-four.

Anna felt pretty much the same. She kept looking from Nikki to Lena, trying to spot the resemblance. Lena's face was rounder... somewhat like Nikki's daughter, Beth. Their coloring was completely different, but Lena resembled Nikki —and Anna—in some intangible way.

She let her gaze travel over Lena from head to toe, noting her clothes. They were much nicer than Anna's comfortable jeans and slouchy sweater. Lena wore a fitted wool coat in a shade of pale gray that seemed to make her green eyes shine brighter. Her hat and scarf were brightly colored, but not in a garish way; they were each made from richly dyed, high-quality wool. She was even wearing high heels. Anna didn't even *own* high heels.

She shot a glance at Nikki, who was still talking... but it was a completely incoherent babble that barely made sense. When Lena finally opened *her* mouth, though, her words were crystal clear.

"No." Lena held up one gloved hand against the onslaught of explanations from her sister. "Nope. Give me a second to catch my breath here."

Lena dropped her hand and began pulling off layers of wool. Nikki moved to help her with her coat while Anna opened her mouth and shut it again, staring like a fish. Somewhere in the back of her mind, she hoped that she would recover her powers of speech before any of her other long-lost relatives appeared.

No, you're the long-lost relative, she remembered. *You're not in Bluebird Bay anymore.*

She was in their town now.

Lena tossed her hat and scarf on the couch and made a beeline for the table, where she sat in Nikki's chair and proceeded to eat her feelings... and the rest of Nikki's breakfast.

After a few bites, she glanced up at Anna, opened her mouth as if to speak, shook her head, and looked away.

Nikki offered her the last of the berry compote she had made and Lena thanked her before dumping it onto the remnants of the waffles.

"I think this calls for a refill," she croaked, holding out Nikki's empty coffee cup.

Nikki took the cup and headed to the kitchen. Anna remained frozen where she stood, torn between competing desires to retreat to the guest room or pepper Lena with a barrage of questions.

Curiosity kept her from the former and empathy stopped her from the latter. She felt for Lena... at least Anna knew this meeting was coming–if not today, soon.

Lena had been completely blindsided and she definitely looked the part.

Nikki set a mug of coffee down in front of her sister and took a seat at the table.

"I was going to tell you today," she said. "It was super last minute."

Anna raised her hand, still hovering at the edge of the room. "My fault on that front."

"I didn't know you were coming by, or I'd have told you for sure," Nikki told Lena.

Lena let out a snort of laughter that reminded Anna of herself.

God, this was going to take some getting used to. Why did the similarities freak her out so much? There must be similar shared traits between her and her Sullivan sisters, but Anna never noticed them. They had spent their whole lives together...They were just themselves, Steph and Cee-cee. She knew them too well to even really *see* them anymore, certainly not with fresh eyes. That was even beginning to happen with Nikki. But Lena...

"It's supposed to drop below freezing tonight," Lena was saying. "When you didn't answer, I figured you were still in Bluebird Bay with your new guy. I was just stopping by to turn on the heat and make sure your pipes didn't freeze."

"Thank you." Nikki's words were heavy with guilt. She looked over at Anna. "Come sit down, Anna. Please."

Anna gingerly claimed a seat at the table, leaving an empty chair between her and Lena.

Lena pushed her plate away and leaned towards Nikki. "Does the Axis of Evil know yet?"

Nikki shook her head, and Anna blinked in confusion.

"The Axis of—" She broke off as it dawned on her, and a bubble of laughter broke from her lips. "Oh my God, do you mean Jack and Gayle?"

"Yes," said Nikki with a wry smile. Her forehead was still furrowed with worry.

"That's our pet name for them," Lena said, speaking directly to Anna for the first time. "Our *secret* pet name. And snitches get stitches," she added with an exaggerated, menacing scowl, "so don't tattle on us about it when you meet them."

"I won't," Anna said, still chuckling. "I promise. Nikki and I were just talking about how to break it to them in a way that wouldn't freak them out."

"Oh, yeah, that's definitely not going to happen." Lena looked down at her plate, sopping up the last of the melted butter and maple syrup. "Freaking out over stuff Nikki does is kind of their whole brand. She's the baby, after all."

A nearly forty-year-old baby, Anna thought. *No wonder Nikki needed some space.*

Nikki busied herself with cleanup even as Lena forked up her last bite of food.

"Stay here," Nikki ordered the both of them, still looking shell-shocked. "I'll make more coffee." She grabbed her phone and hurried into the kitchen. A moment later, the strains of a familiar Duran Duran song began to play.

Loudly.

Lena leaned in and whispered, "She's having a freak out

and doesn't want us to hear her talking to herself. That's what she does. How has she been? Really?"

"What do you mean?" Anna asked.

"Everything that happened with Steve, being held at gunpoint, the father of her daughter, dead on her floor... she told me about it like it happened to someone else. Totally detached. Like it didn't even affect her, which isn't possible. So...how is she really?"

Anna shot a glance into the kitchen where their younger sister stood at the sink, scrubbing the breakfast dishes to within an inch of their lives.

"She seemed more relieved than anything, honestly," Anna said quietly. "She was so scared for a while, after the break-in, and that mangled bird that was left on her porch. I think part of her wondered if she was crazy or something and it was all just a coincidence."

"The what and the *what*?" Lena demanded, eyes popping wide.

Crap.

"Ah, geez..." Anna raked a hand through her hair with a sigh. "Look, Lena. Some other stuff happened leading up to the suicide. I guess she didn't get a chance to mention—"

"Yeah, a break-in and a mangled bird apparently didn't make the cut of the week's highlights," Lena mumbled. "She didn't tell me because she knew I would have shown up two hours later to take her home."

Nikki spared them a quick look over her shoulder and went back to scrubbing dishes, studiously ignoring them as Duran Duran played on.

"Anyway," Anna pressed on, "when he finally *did* show

up, and then...the events transpired," she found it hard to talk about that night, "she was shaken up at first, but after a week or two, it was like she could finally breathe again. I think she was so used to looking over her shoulder or worrying about when he might get out and what could happen."

"And no wonder. He was a monster," Lena muttered under her breath. "Good riddance to bad rubbish."

"More than anything, she was worried about how it would affect Beth. But they worked things out when she showed up in town. It was tense for a bit, but by Thanksgiving, they were solid."

"Thanksgiving with the Sullivans in Bluebird Bay." Lena leaned back and bit her lip. "I don't mean to be rude, but sitting here with you feels like a fever dream. You just look *so* much like her. And Dad."

"So I've heard."

Lena let out a sigh. "I'm sorry. Really. I can't imagine being on the other end of all this."

"Yeah..." Anna looked down at her hands. "I was in denial for a while. My sisters sprang it on me and I went off on them. I wanted nothing to do with Nikki. I wouldn't even talk to her. But eventually, I let her in." Anna looked up with a tight smile. "She was persistent."

Lena was looking off into the distance. "Do you ever wish you could talk to your mom about all this?"

"Only every day."

Lena's lips tipped into a sad smile. "Sorry. Stupid question."

"It's fine. You're still trying to digest it all," Anna assured her before continuing. "My sisters actually found our mom's journal. From...back then. My dad left it for us."

"Really?" Lena's eyebrows shot up. "Did you read it?"

"We did."

"And?"

"It was hard at first, but... it helped. It helped us understand her and our dad and their marriage. She had really severe postpartum depression. Not that she knew to call it that back then. Pop was working long hours, and Mom was so lost. She finally started feeling better when she started part-time at the local library, which is where she met your dad."

Our dad.

"I still can't wrap my head around it," Lena admitted with a shrug. "That he would cheat on my mom. And with someone else's wife. Someone's *mother*. He's not that guy."

"And my mom wasn't that woman. But then, in that moment, they were. For what it's worth, I think it was the only time. Just Eric."

"Maybe they were in love..." Lena blanched. "Yuck. Let's talk about something else. Those waffles are thinking about making a reappearance. Tell me about your sisters," she added in a rush. "What are they like?"

Anna gave Lena a smile, grateful for the easy question.

"They're amazing," she said honestly. "Brilliant, each in their own special way. Supportive. I had a cancer scare last year... I don't know what I would have done without them. Cee-cee's the oldest. She did the Stepford wife thing for a long time before that ended in spectacular fashion when he left her for their realtor. Now, she has her own chain of cupcake shops and an amazing fiancé. Stephanie's a veterinarian, mostly retired now. Her son Todd took over her practice. I have five nieces and nephews. On the Sullivan side, that is."

"No kids?"

"Nope."

"Me neither," Lena said, her tone unreadable.

"I do sort of have a grandson," Anna said brightly. "His name is Teddy."

At Lena's questioning look, she continued.

"My boyfriend Beckett. We live together, and his grandson spends a lot of time with us. I can't believe my luck. I skipped the decades of motherhood, and now I still get to do the easy, fun part. My sisters aren't even grandmothers yet – though Cee-cee will be, in a few months."

"You were too busy jet-setting around the world to start a family. I've seen your photos. I might have stalked you online a little bit," Lena admitted with an impish smile. "You're really talented. Those shots of the mother wolf with her pups...oh man. Those got me."

Funny. Those were some of Anna's favorites too.

"Thanks. I really love what I do. I don't miss the constant travel, though. It was fun in my twenties and thirties, but these days? I just want to be closer to family. And then there's Beckett and Teddy. I mostly just do local photography now for a wildlife sanctuary, and freelance work when I get some great shots while hiking. What do you do?"

"I'm a personal assist-" Lena's eyes went wide as she broke off. "Oh my God." She sprang up from her seat. "I was only supposed to run in and turn on the heat. I've got to go!"

"Wait!" Nikki came rushing in from the kitchen, soap bubbles dripping from her hands. "Where are you going?"

"I'm supposed to meet Freddie at the gallery at nine with a macha and three raspberry macarons!" Lena exclaimed as she pulled on her coat. "He's going to kill me."

"But what are we going to do about Jack and Gayle? Should we tell Dad first, or—?"

"'*We*'?" Lena snorted. "There is no '*we*' here. Well, there's *that* we," she gestured vaguely between Nikki and Anna, "but there is no *me* 'we'."

"But it would just be way easier if we all tell them tog—"

"I would do anything for love, little sister," Lena said, quoting the old Meatloaf song on her way to the door, "but I won't do that. Just let me know once you've told them...if you live through it. After a proper cooling off period, I'm happy to have everyone over to my house for dinner, though. Sorry and I love you!"

Nikki opened her mouth to protest, and Lena cut her off, already halfway out the door.

"Don't worry. If I don't have time to make chicken pot pie, I'll just get takeout."

Then she was gone, and Nikki and Anna were left staring after her.

"Well, that was interesting," Anna finally managed.

"Yeah. One down, I guess." Nikki slumped onto her charmingly hideous yellow couch. "Two to go."

They stayed like that in silence, each of them lost in their own thoughts, until Anna finally spoke.

"Look, if you don't want to do this, I can go back home. Give you some time to talk to Gayle and Jack. Or not. You can just bring your dad to Bluebird Bay, maybe?"

"Nope," Nikki said, shaking her head resolutely. "Even if

you weren't here, this would need to happen. I've got to start pushing back with them and letting them know that they aren't the boss of me. And there is no time like the present. Dad wanted to meet you, and you're here now. It's going to happen whether the twins like it or not. I need a hot shower and a good long think. I'll have a plan for us by the time I get dressed. Promise."

She stood and padded out of the room, down the hall.

"Whew," Anna mumbled as she slumped lower into her seat. If it was all this exhausting and they were just getting started, her time in Cherry Blossom Point was going to be draining.

She needed a pick-me-up. With that in mind, she dug the phone from her pocket to call Beckett, her heart already warming at the thought.

Beckett.

He was such a blessing. He'd handled her sudden decision to leave town like a champ. When he'd asked if she wanted him to go with her, she'd told him that she needed to do this alone, reminding him how difficult she could be when she was dealing with hard life stuff. She tried not to, but sometimes she even lashed out. More often, she shut down. Hell, she'd almost driven Nikki away. The thought of driving Beckett away was almost too much to bear.

"Not possible," Beckett had told her with a kiss, *"but I support your decision. If you change your mind at any point, just tell me and I'll be there."*

She only planned to stay a couple weeks, and that was the best-case scenario. Worst case was that she left town in a couple days. It all depended on how things went with Eric.

Her stomach rolled and she shoved that thought aside as

she tapped Beckett's name on her speed-dial screen. He answered on the first ring.

"Well?" he asked in lieu of hello. "How's it going in Cherry Blossom Point today? Still the town's best kept secret?"

Anna chuckled. "Funny you should ask..."

3

LENA

LENA FUMBLED for her keys as she hurried away from Nikki's house. This day had gotten real *Twilight Zone* real quick.

Seeing pictures of Anna had been weird enough — she looked *so* much like Nikki — but seeing her in person was a whole other ball game. Her resemblance to their father was almost startling. Lena had even seen glimpses of Jack and Gayle in Anna's shifting expressions...the twist of her mouth, the line that appeared between her eyes when she frowned. She was a complete stranger, and yet so eerily familiar.

"Stalking her online didn't help at all," Lena muttered as she started her car. The curiosity had been too much for Lena; she had combed through pictures of Anna to find similarities between her and the Merrills. Then she had been genuinely intrigued by Anna's photography and had continued down the rabbit hole. Pictures of Anna at awards shows and art galleries all mixed together with her photos of polar bears and wolves and rare birds. By the time Lena met her in person, it felt a little like meeting a movie star....one with her father's eyes.

And nose.

And hair.

Good lord, she was a real chip off the old block. Anna and Nikki both were, in different ways.

Lena had always been the odd one out. Jack and Gayle both bore a strong resemblance to their mother, and Nikki was a Merrill through and through. Lena, with the teal green eyes and golden hair she'd inherited from their grandmother, didn't bear a striking resemblance to anyone in her immediate family. Even her features were different; her face was rounder than her sisters', her nose small and upturned. She was the shortest one in the family by inches (hence the constant heels) and the curviest. Her sisters had openly envied her full figure when they were young. No amount of padding would give them a fraction of the cleavage that Lena spent her teenage years trying to cover up. As they'd gotten older, though, Gayle and Nikki had stayed trim with what seemed like little effort while Lena fought a constant battle to ensure that her wardrobe would fit her for another year. When she was younger, her blonde hair nearly white, she had secretly been convinced she was adopted... until she'd seen an old photo album that had belonged to her grandmother. Other than the hair — Lena had inherited her father's curls — she was the spitting image of her mom's mom.

Thoughts of her mother sent a wave of grief rolling over her.

Lord, but she missed that woman. Two years after her death, the grief was still so close to the surface. Lena was fiercely grateful that Eric was still with them...and at the same time, she felt so angry with him for a lifetime of secrets. He had cheated on his wife. Worse than that, he had known that his liaison had resulted in another child. One who grew up only two hours away from them. He had known, and he had never told them. Not until after their mother's death. Wanda had made him promise not to tell because she had tried to block it out. The kids knowing would make it all the more real. If Lena was honest with herself, that decision hurt too, but it was much less complicated to direct her anger towards the parent who was still alive.

Lena's phone rang, and she hazarded a quick glance as she drove.

Gayle.

No friggin' way was she answering.

She let the phone ring until it went to voicemail. It probably wasn't anything important, anyway. Gayle called her a few times a week to chit-chat about nothing. The latest town gossip that she overheard at her bar, The Milky Thistle. Gripes about her husband, Rex, whom she refused to leave. News from Maddy and Reid, her grown children who had gone out of state for college and settled far away after graduation. Lena didn't have the ability to manage small talk right now. Not with Anna weighing on her mind.

Her brain conjured a thousand outcomes of Nikki telling them about Anna's presence in Cherry Blossom Point, most of them bad. Would they still be so easily dismissive if they met Anna in person? Or worse, overtly hostile? Maybe the family resemblance would make it hard to shoot her down...

She knew one thing for sure: the apple didn't fall too far from the tree on the whole secret keeping thing. She wouldn't *tell* the twins, but she had a terrible poker face. She couldn't talk to Gayle until Nikki broke the news. Look at how Bethy had *known* that something was going on with Nikki after talking to her. She hadn't even needed to see Lena's face! Her fumbling on the phone had been enough.

No, she would do well to just avoid the twins altogether for the immediate future. She couldn't hide her emotions on a good day. After the shock she'd just had, they would know instantly that something was amiss.

She pulled up to the curb in front of Sadie's Cafe. Her former sister-in-law made the best—okay, the best and *only*—French macarons in town. And if Freddie demanded matcha and macarons? It was Lena's job to ensure he got them...and anything else her boss wanted.

She let out a sigh.

She still couldn't quite figure out how she had wound up as an overworked assistant in her mid-forties when she'd dreamed of so much more. But that was a question for another day.

Family crisis today. Existential crisis tomorrow.

"Get it together or you're going to be late," she muttered as she stepped out of the car into the chilly morning air.

She ran into the cafe and stood tapping a nervous heel on the tile floor as the line moved at a snail's pace. This was so not good.

She checked her phone, swiping past texts from Nikki and Gayle, and noted the time.

No doubt about it now, she was definitely going to be late. Luckily, so was Freddie.

Usually. Not that it stopped him from pitching a fit on the rare occasion that *she* showed up late. But that was only if he was in one of his tempers, in which case, he might even start throwing things. Hopefully he was in a good mood today. If not, it might be the day that Lena finally threw something *back*.

"Hi, Lena," Sadie greeted her as she moved to the front of the line. "What can I get you?"

The whole family still got on well with Jack's ex-wife, and Lena gave her a sincere smile. "Hey, Sadie. Good to see you! I just need six raspberry macarons and a large matcha, please. With soy milk."

Sadie wrinkled her nose. "Ah, sorry, friend. No raspberry today."

"No," Lena groaned.

"We have strawberry," Sadie said with a chuckle, well aware of Freddie's diva-ish requests. "I swear they're delicious."

Would Freddie even notice the difference?

"Okay. Six strawberry, please."

"Coming right up. I have a couple new flavors, too. I'll throw one of each in for you to try. There's a ginger – tell me if it's too spicy – and I may have finally perfected pistachio."

"Thanks!"

Sadie nodded and handed over the box of macarons. Lena paid and turned to go. She was halfway to the door when it swung open and Gayle walked in.

"Hey!" Her big sister greeted her with a smile. "I tried to call you a couple minutes ago."

Heat rushed to her face as she tried not to make eye contact.

Crap, crap, crap.

Act normal. Act normal!

She kept her head down, clicking quickly past; her heels made the most infernal racket on the tile floor.

"Gotta go," she muttered. "I really need to...go to the bathroom."

There was a long pause. "Sadie has a bathroom here." Gayle sounded bewildered, but Lena wasn't about to stick around long enough for explanations.

She raced out the door and down the sidewalk, leaving her car where it was. The art gallery was only a block away. Even in heels, it was quicker to hoof it than to repark the car. Matcha dripped down her wrist as she raced up the street, ten minutes late. She opened the door to the gallery, barely juggling the cup of matcha with the box of macarons... and ran straight into Owen McKenna. She could feel the delicate shells of the macarons crackle as the box crumpled against his chest.

"Ah!" Owen said, his tone a jumble of surprise and amusement and pain. "That's hot."

"Crap," Lena said, watching in horror as green matcha spread across his white cotton shirt. "I am so sorry, Owen."

He ushered her inside with a gentle touch to her back, and then he gingerly took the phone and crumpled box from one hand and the depleted matcha from the other, setting them down on a nearby table.

"Take a breath, darling. Nothing's on fire. It was a bit of a shocker, but I'm not truly burned."

Lena laughed and looked up into Owen's blue eyes, which did absolutely nothing to regulate her nervous system. If anything, Lena's heart beat even faster.

Get a grip, she told herself sternly. *You have known this man for over 30 years, through braces and puberty and high school angst. How is it that he still makes you feel like a tongue-tied teenager?*

But God help her, the man was gorgeous. Black Irish, with dark hair and sea-blue eyes. When he opened his mouth to speak, it only made things worse. The man was unfailingly warm, and the faint Irish accent that remained after spending the majority of his life in Maine still made Lena weak in the knees. Her and every other woman in Cherry Blossom Point.

Get it together, Lena.

"Are you alright?" Owen asked.

"I'm fine." Lena looked away from those dangerous blue eyes, examining the large pea-green stain on his shirt. "Are *you*? You're the one with a chest covered in hot green soy milk."

"I'm fine. It wasn't that hot." He chuckled. "But what's the rush?"

"I'm late. I was supposed to meet him at nine."

"As if Freddie ever arrives anywhere on time. He's not even here yet."

Just as Owen said his name — or rather, the nickname that Frederick loathed — Lena's employer strolled into the gallery with two large canvases in hand. It was nearly December, and yet he wore only a pair of jeans and a t-shirt with David Bowie's face printed on the front. His blond hair was coiffed in a swoop that left a lock hanging over one of his green eyes...that Lena knew came courtesy of colored contacts.

One bleached brow shot up as he took in the mess with a glance and shook his head.

"Luckily for you, the mood for matcha and macarons has passed."

"Good morning, Frederick," Lena replied dismally.

He leaned the canvases against the wall. "I have five more paintings at my place we need to pick up and then we need to help Sheree decide where to hang them." He jerked a thumb toward Owen. "Poor-man's Bradley Cooper here took up the whole front room of the gallery with his Christmas bric-a-brac collection, so I've been relegated to the back like persona non grata. Get your car and meet me at home. Replace my breakfast while you're at it. I'll have a chai and one of those chocolate croissants."

So... the cafe on the other side of town, thought Lena with an internal grimace. *Lovely.* Well, at least she wouldn't run into Gayle over there.

"I'll be at your place in half an hour," she promised her boss as he sidestepped a puddle of matcha, nose wrinkled.

"Always a pleasure, Freddie," Owen said sardonically.

"You were terrible in *Silver Linings Playbook*, by the way," Freddie stage-whispered on his way out the door. Owen just chuckled.

Her boss harbored a multitude of jealousies toward Owen and was forever taking shots at him—but the truth was, Bradley Cooper couldn't hold a candle to Owen McKenna. Not that she would ever tell him that. He just oozed charisma and warmth in a way that made everyone he was talking to feel special. But despite the fact that she'd fantasized more than once about him dipping her backwards and kissing her like his life depended on it, she knew it was a pipe dream. He could have any woman he wanted, and he had no qualms about testing that theory. She rarely saw him with the same woman twice. Not to mention, she was pretty sure he thought of her like a little sister. Cute, harmless, fun to have around.

That sounds more like a puppy than a sister, she realized with a wince.

Point being, there was not now, nor would there ever be, anything more than loving friendship between her and Owen McKenna.

She shoved aside the little stab of disappointment as she leaned against the wall with a sigh, snatching up the crumpled little box of macarons.

Sure, they were crushed, but at least the box had kept them safe from Freddie's leaf-and-legume drink disaster.

She popped a broken ginger macaron into her mouth and sighed.

Divine.

Lena held out the box to Owen.

"Want one?" she asked with a full mouth.

"No thanks," Owen replied as he stripped off his stained shirt and used a dry section to wipe at the damp patch of green that had seeped through to the white t-shirt he was wearing underneath.

Lena stopped chewing.

Owen in an untucked button-down and jeans was bad enough. Owen in a second-skin, threadbare t-shirt so thin she could see through it, was just too much. His six-foot frame was leanly muscled in a way that made her want to run her hands over him. Before becoming a glassblower he'd been a tattoo artist, and he had a smattering of tattoos on his upper arms and across his chest. She'd seen most of them up close at various picnics and beach trips, but that didn't make it any easier to tear her gaze away.

"Your loss," she managed as she swallowed. "Sadie has perfected the pistachio."

Her phone buzzed from the nearby table and Owen leaned in to peer down at it.

"Gayle wants to know if you ate something off for breakfast and asks if you made it to the bathroom in time?"

Of course she did.

A hot flush crept up Lena's cheeks and she cleared her throat.

"I wasn't—I just—"

"Bit of a day already, yeah?" Owen asked gently. He dropped his dirty shirt to the floor and moved it around with one foot, sopping up the matcha that had spilled as he continued. "Good news is, it can only get better from here."

"I met my half-sister this morning," she blurted. "Anna."

Owen looked up in surprise and let out a low whistle.

"And I thought getting insulted by Freddie was tough."

"That's just another day," Lena replied lightly. "The Anna thing...that's going to be a sticky situation."

Owen frowned at her, but his frowns never lasted long.

"That's a lot of sticky stuff in one day," he said, bending to grab his shirt. "I hope the rest of it goes easier for you." He leaned in and tugged at one of her curls in the same gentle, teasing way he had when they were twelve years old and he was the new boy in school. Three decades plus and the gesture still made her heart race.

Damn it.

He didn't mean anything by it, she reminded herself crossly. She had watched him flirt with anything with a pulse for the entirety of their friendship. She had told her now-exes time and again that it was nothing...it came to him as naturally as breathing. He treated the seventy-year-old waitress at their favorite diner the same way, just to see her smile.

Reality check complete, she nodded and managed a smile.

"I don't think it can get any worse."

"That's the spirit. It's all up from here," Owen agreed. He cleared his throat and took a step back. "Sorry, I've got to go. I've got a commission that I'm already behind on. See you later in the week for a meal, yeah?"

"Yup, sounds good." Lena's fingers were creating new dents in the already crumpled pastry box as Owen left, giving her a light peck on the cheek on his way out the door.

She went into the back to wash sugar and matcha from her hands and said a quick hello to Sheree, who was doing some paperwork before the gallery officially opened at ten. When Lena walked back out into the front room, she stopped short with a gasp.

In all the rushing around and clumsy confusion, she hadn't even noticed the display of Owen's latest collection.

It was stunning. Delicate orbs in swirls of color that danced in the morning light hung from birch tree branches, creating a kaleidoscope against the while walls. A table with artfully arranged glass menorahs and candlesticks in blues and whites that should've felt colder than the warmer color palettes but somehow exuded warmth and joy… Her favorites were the plates in gold, silver, red, and green, each one as delicately textured as a poppy flower, an array of ombre that bloomed from richly-colored centers to the plates' clear-glass edges.

Lena saw in her mind's eye how the displays would catch the late afternoon light through the front windows just when the gallery was at its busiest. Owen was a master of color and light, and Sheree had given him the perfect foil for it in this room.

"Christmas bric-a-brac," she muttered under her breath. "Freddie, you're an idiot sometimes."

An ember of excitement bloomed in her belly the way it always did when she saw genius. This would be it. This would be the year that the rest of the world saw what Lena already knew. Owen was extraordinary.

He needed to go national. Get his stuff seen by—

Her phone buzzed and she looked reluctantly away from the display with a sigh.

I'm not paying you to moon over the eye candy at Sheree's. Get over here. PRONTO.

Lena muttered a curse under her breath and shoved the phone back into her purse. She hoped that Owen was right and that the day would get better from here. Anna's face flashed through her mind, followed by Gayle and Jack's, and Lena let out a groan.

She didn't have high hopes.

4

NIKKI

"HEY, SWEETHEART." Just the sound of Mateo's voice was soothing. "I'm so glad you called, I was just thinking about you. How's it going?"

"Ugh, I don't even know anymore." Nikki sat on the edge of her bed wrapped in a towel as she filled him in on the morning with Lena and Anna. Her hair was still dripping water from the shower as she finished. "Point being, I don't know what I'm doing. Or how I'm doing. Or why I'm doing... what I'm doing. What was the question?" she asked with a semi-hysterical chuckle.

"That good, huh?"

"I'm scattered. Honestly, I feel terrified."

"What are you so scared of?"

Good lord, Mateo, Nikki thought. *What am I* not *scared of?*

"Let's see...I'm scared that Gayle will hate me, that Anna will leave, that my dad will get his feelings hurt," she began aloud as she ticked off the list on her fingers. "Annnd, I'm worried that Jack will drive Anna away and ruin Christmas for everyone." She paused for a long moment. "There's more, I'm just already sick of listening to myself, so I'll stop now. Point is, there's already this rift, you know? Jack and Gayle on one side — it was always them and Mom — with me and Dad on the other... Lena kind of hang-gliding back and forth between us."

"That big of a rift, huh?"

She could hear the smile in his voice and found her lips twitching as she smiled in response.

"You think I'm being dramatic."

"I think that maybe you're blowing things out of proportion and taking responsibility for things that aren't on you," he said gently.

"Jack and Gayle are going to be furious with me. That's a given. What if they're mad at Dad too? For wanting to meet Anna? What if they hold it against him for the rest of his life, like he's choosing Anna over them?"

"They can handle it, Nikki. They're old enough to be grandparents, for Pete's sake. It's time for everyone to grow up, don't you think?"

"I do," she said dubiously, "but seems like if that was going to happen, it'd have happened already, right? I've got to face facts here. This is going to be a fight."

War was more like it, but she knew Mateo already thought she was overselling it. If he only knew. She made a mental note to invite him to visit in a couple weeks...once the initial furor died down or Anna was safely out of range. No point in bringing Mateo into the line of fire in the middle of this.

"One thing you have to remember, Nikki. It's not your job to make sure everyone is happy. You have to do what *you* think is right. The rest is out of your hands. *They* get to choose how they react to it."

She considered his words for a long moment, pinching the bridge of her nose between her thumb and forefinger.

Was bringing Anna to Cherry Blossom Point a mistake? Letting her tag along without taking the time to prepare everyone first certainly felt like a mistake right now. But would Nikki look back on it as a *happy* mistake...one that brought everyone together in the end? Or would this be the mistake that truly tore their family apart?

"Nikki? Are you still there?"

"I'm here. Just wondering if I should've called Gayle before we got here."

"Just playing devil's advocate here, because I'm not sure of the right answer either. But don't you think she'd have talked you out of it? Then you wouldn't be being true to yourself and doing what *you* thought was right."

He had a point there. History had proven time and time again that she didn't have the backbone to stand up to her much older sister, nevermind withstand a coordinated attack from the Axis of Evil.

"That's true," she murmured.

"Trust your gut, Nikki. You know what the right thing to do is from here, deep down. Tell me, what *feels right*?"

"Bringing Anna over to Dad's house," she answered instantly, trying not to think before answering and speaking from the heart. "Surprising Dad with Anna is the best gift he could ever receive." Eric loved surprises, and this one trumped every Christmas gift he had ever received, times a thousand.

"Then do that," Mateo encouraged her.

Fear gripped her heart in its icy fingers. "And what about the twins?"

"They're your siblings, not your keepers. Stand strong behind your decision and don't let them make you second-guess yourself. You can do this."

Nikki took a long, slow breath in and let it out in a rush.

"Thank you. It must all seem silly simple from your perspective. I just... you know how, when you've known people your whole life, you fall into these roles? Even if you're a completely different person than you were decades before, when all the roles were cast?"

"Believe me, I know a little something about dysfunctional family dynamics," Mateo reminded her. Understatement of the decade. The man had gone through hell and come out unscathed. Or, more accurately, he had come out very deeply scathed... but had done the work to heal a lot of those wounds long before Nikki had ever met him. "I also know that you can choose to break out of them," Mateo continued. "You can be the pioneer. The family Magellan, forging a path into the unknown. You might find that they don't like their roles either, these overbearing older siblings of yours. Who knows? Maybe if you take charge, it will free them up to make a positive shift, too."

"I miss you," Nikki said impulsively. "I miss you so much already."

"Just name the date and I'm there," Mateo said in a warm voice. "No rush. Family comes first. But whenever you're ready. Tara's spending her winter break in South Carolina with her mom and that side of the family, so I'm free as a bird. I'm excited to see your town. And you. Mostly you."

A rush of affection ran through her, and she found herself grinning.

"How's the house coming?" she asked, changing the subject to a happier topic.

"Now that you mention it, I just finished painting the kitchen today," Mateo replied. "That 'Winter Sky' gray you picked out, the one that was just a shade darker than white."

"The pale silvery one," Nikki remembered.

"Yeah," he confirmed. "It looks good."

"If there's one thing I know, it's kitchens. That's the best thing about being home. I can't wait to cook you a meal in my own kitchen."

"I've seen what you can do with limited resources. I can only imagine what you can do on your home turf."

"I'll knock your socks off," she promised.

"You've done that already," Mateo told her solemnly. Then, in a lighter tone, he said, "But hey, I'll put on a new pair."

Nikki laughed.

"How's Beth doing?" he asked.

"Settling in," Nikki replied. "She's enjoying her classes, taking Italian this semester... she wants to study abroad."

"Sounds like the perfect excuse for us to take a trip to Italy."

"That sounds like a dream."

They would need to get a real vacation rental instead of a hotel. Something with a kitchen... Restaurants were all well and good, but if Nikki visited Italy, she would need a space to cook up all of the amazing ingredients that lined the streets.

"You're thinking of the food, aren't you?"

"It's Italy! What else would I be thinking about?"

Mateo chuckled.

"The company sounds okay, too," she teased. Then she sighed. "I should probably go. Anna is waiting on me to tell her the grand plan, and I still have to come up with one. I'll call you tonight?"

"Sounds good."

Nikki tugged on a pair of faded jeans and a sweatshirt and then headed out to the living room, where Anna sat flipping through an old magazine.

"Feel like whipping up your famous lasagna?" Nikki asked on pure impulse.

"For what?" Anna asked, looking up. "Tired of cooking for me already?"

She sucked in a breath and blew it out in a rush.

"I thought we could bring it to my...um, our father's house for dinner."

5

ANNA

"Okay. Cool. So...here we are," Anna mumbled as she stared at the cheerily lit cape cod-style home just yards away.

The sun had nearly set, and she and Nikki were seated in Nikki's car outside her — their — father's house, lasagna in tow.

"Yup, here we are," Nikki parroted as she took her keys from the ignition and promptly dropped them to the floor. Anna realized with a start that her sister's hands were shaking.

At least she wasn't the only nervous wreck.

"This is the right move," Nikki said, nodding emphatically. Anna wasn't sure if she was talking more to Anna or to herself. "He's going to be so happy. You both want to meet each other. It's ridiculous to keep hiding just because the twins might get angry."

"What if he changed his mind since you last spoke to him? Or what if we give him a heart attack?"

"That's not going to happen. I remember the wistful look in his eyes when he told us about you. The regret. '*Maybe I'll still get the chance to meet her someday,'* he said, after the twins had stormed out in a huff. It's going to be amazing," Nikki assured her as she reached down and fished her keys off of the floor of the car. "Ready?"

Nope.

"Yep," Anna said with a single, quick nod.

Nikki got out of the car and circled around to open the door for Anna. She led the way up the path to the family house and opened the front door.

"Dad?" Nikki called out. "I'm back!"

"Ah, my baby girl is home!" a male baritone called from the den. "It is so good to hear your voice! I'll be out in a jiffy. I want to hear everything. Tell me about your s—"

Eric stopped short as he came around the corner and caught sight of Anna. He stared at her, stunned, as she stared back in silence. For a brief moment, she worried she had been right to fear a heart attack.

"I brought you a souvenir from Bluebird Bay," Nikki murmured.

But Anna barely heard her through the rush of blood in her ears.

"Anna," her biological father whispered an instant before his voice hitched and his face crumpled. She stood frozen to the spot in the unfamiliar living room, lasagna in hand, as he wept. The whole house smelled like cinnamon, she realized inanely. Was she having a stroke?

Was *he*?

Eric stood stock still, tears pouring down his face, staring right back at her.

"I, um, I made lasagna." She thrust the casserole pan towards Eric. Nikki took it from her and disappeared.

"I swear it, you look just like Rosie," Eric whispered. He walked forward slowly, and raised one hand as if to touch her face... then stopped, and let the hand drop.

"Hi, I'm, um, I'm Anna," she said stupidly, and stuck out her own hand in greeting. Eric took it in both of his. His hands were strong, and surprisingly soft. The man was so much smaller in person than he had been in her mind... his eyes were level with hers, and just the same blend of green and gold. He had her long nose and her pointed chin... or rather, *she* had *his*. Eric's hair had gone gray, but it was still fiercely curly.

"I'm so happy you're here." Eric's voice was choked with emotion.

"I put the lasagna in the oven on low," Nikki called out as she walked back in. Her voice faltered as she looked between Eric and Anna. "To keep warm."

Eric released Anna's hand and pulled Nikki into a hug.

"I missed you so much, chickadee," he told his youngest daughter. "Thank you for coming. And for bringing her with you." He straightened up and turned to Anna. "I had always hoped—always had this tiny sliver of hope— that I might meet you someday. I was always looking for you. Not, um, not on purpose. I promised..." He paused, running a hand through his hair. He looked terrified. "Every county fair that we went to, every field trip or day at the beach, I would always find myself scanning the crowd without even meaning to. You were always there, in the back of my mind. I tried not to think about it. It hurt too much. But you're here. You're really here."

Eric pulled a handkerchief from his pocket and blew his nose loudly. Then, he mopped up his eyes with one sleeve.

"Come in, please. No more tears. This is a celebration!"

He turned on the dining room light with the flick of a switch and began pulling delicate, blue-patterned plates from a glass-fronted cabinet.

"If *this* doesn't call for the good china," Eric said as he set the table, "I don't know what does."

Nikki ran in and out, bringing silverware and stemmed glasses and a bottle of cider. Anna stood speechless, watching her biological father's every little gesture with fascination. Though he was excited and moving quickly, his movements were steady and sure. As for herself, Anna stood far from the table for fear of breaking what she was certain had to be the Merrills' wedding china. The last thing she needed was to evoke the ire of Wanda's ghost.

Eric's late wife was everywhere in this house. Her face smiled out from the walls. There was a wedding picture in a silver frame, in the same cabinet as the china plates. Family photos lined the opposite wall. The twins as babies, dark-haired and chubby. Lena with a halo of white-blonde curls. Baby Nikki, front and center in a family photo. In each photo, just behind the children, Wanda seemed to jeer at her. Besides the wedding photo, there were no pictures of Eric. That would make him the photographer in the family.

Interesting.

"Sit down, please," Eric invited.

Anna turned away from the family photos and managed a smile. Despite all of her fears and her wounded heart, she felt a strange sort of joy in his presence. Guilt followed, hot on its heels.

You're still my true dad, Pop, and you always will be.

"I can't believe you made me dinner," Eric said as they all

took their seats at the table. Nikki had raided Eric's kitchen and thrown together a salad in record time. She served it up in silence, and Anna took a huge bite of lasagna to spare herself from speaking. Eric did the same, and followed it with another.

"This is the best lasagna I've ever tasted." He looked at Anna, his face shining with pure and unabashed love.

And suddenly, she was tearing up like a frigging idiot. She feigned a cough and hid her face behind a napkin.

Get a grip! You do not cry in front of strangers. Who even are you right now?

It was no use, though. Her inner child had grabbed the wheel, and that damned kid was having a meltdown.

Eric placed one warm hand over hers and held it there in silence, which only made holding the tears in harder.

She pulled her hand away and buried her face in the fine cloth napkin. Breaking down in front of Eric felt foriegn and scary and awful, but she couldn't seem to stop.

"I am so sorry. I don't know what's wrong with me."

Nikki cleared her throat. "Hey Dad, I forgot the salad dressing. Would you grab the vinaigrette?"

Eric's chair scraped the floor as he stood, and a moment later, Anna heard the kitchen door close. She sunk her face to the table as her little sister reached over and rubbed her back.

"It's okay. You're okay. This is totally normal."

"Not for me, it isn't," Anna shot back with a loud sniffle.

"The bathroom is down the hall to the right if you want to take a minute," Nikki offered with quiet empathy.

"Thanks."

She found her way to the bathroom, where she closed the door, sank to her knees, and released the wracking sobs that had hijacked her body like some sort of annoying, super wimpy demon.

After a full minute of that, she let out a shuddering breath.

"Okay. You got this. No problemo."

She stood and leaned into the sink, taking a few moments to splash cold water on her face. The reddened eyes that peered back from the mirror were so similar to Eric's that she almost started to cry again.

"Cut the crap, get out there, and eat some lasagna, Sullivan. You faced down an armed psychopath last month. You can handle sitting across the table for a meal with a sweet old man."

She took a long, shuddering breath and opened the door.

"Dad and I were just talking about your work," Nikki said brightly as Anna walked back into the dining room.

Anna glanced towards Eric and away. His expression was one she might expect to see from a man holding his newborn baby for the first time. But here they were, fifty years late, and apparently starting from scratch.

"I love your photography," Eric said earnestly. "Lena showed me a few months back, on the computer. Those shots of the Iberian Lynx and her cubs were so incredibly beautiful."

"Thank you," Anna said, hazarding a glance at her biological father.

"The birds are my favorites, though." The smile he gave her was pure joy, and the last of her tears evaporated under the light that shone from his eyes.

"We saw all of your recent work, too," he continued. "That close-up of the puffin with three silver fish coming out the side of its beak, wow. The detail that you captured was just phenomenal. The orange and white striation on its beak, the texture of its feathers, even the *expression* on its face. Amazing, Anna, really."

Anna blinked. Her own parents hadn't even seen most of her work. They'd both offered the occasional word of praise, but it was always tempered by low-key irritation at her choice of career, which took her out of town more than they'd have liked. Even those *thoughts* made her stomach churn with guilt.

Pop had raised her as his own, loved her, treated her like his own flesh and blood. The man sitting across from her was a stranger, and she was already comparing them.

What a traitor.

Eric hadn't been the one working extra hours to pay for the ear surgery insurance had refused to cover. Eric hadn't been the one clapping and whistling at her God-awful middle school chorus concert after she'd butchered her solo performance of Little Drummer Boy. Eric hadn't been the one by her mother's side when the chemo made her so sick she couldn't even eat a piece of toast without vomiting.

He and Pop were *not* the same.

But does that mean you can't learn to love this man too? Appreciate what gifts he might bring to your life and vice versa?

She shot a glance at Nikki, who was smiling gently in her general direction. Her sweet, kind, persistent little sister. Anna could hardly remember what it was like not having her around, and it had only been a couple months.

She had come to Cherry Blossom Point to meet her father and see if there might be a place for him in her life. So far, so good. She needed to stop looking gift horses in the mouth and start accepting that this whole journey was going to be weird and confusing and painful at times. But if it was anything like the one between her and Nikki, it would be worth it.

Anna took a sip of sweet-tart cider and steadied herself.

"So, Eric, what do you like to do in your free time?" she asked, tipping her lips into a smile.

"Dad's a birder," Nikki said, looking toward Eric. "He always has been, but he *really* got into it after retirement. Right, Dad?"

"I've always been fascinated with flight," Eric said, nodding. "I used to dream of being a pilot. Now I'm content to watch the experts...I don't even try to photograph them anymore. It was an exercise in frustration, nothing but blurred shapes and empty branches. I'll leave that work to the professionals," he added with a wink. "It's no easy task."

She forked up another huge bite of lasagna and shrugged. "A few little tweaks and tips, and anyone can take a good picture. I can show you sometime if you want..."

Eric's eyes went glassy and he blinked hard before nodding. "Yes. Please. I would love that." He paused and then leaned in, brows furrowed. "I wonder if you'd tell me where you found that grasshopper sparrow?"

She set down her fork and swallowed hard. "Wow, you really are up to date on my work. Have you ever seen one in person?"

"I think I've heard them before, but I've never caught a glimpse of one."

"I took that picture in Kennebunk Plains."

"Oh, lovely. I saw vesper sparrows when I was there, and the most beautiful horned lark, but no grasshopper sparrows."

"I haven't gotten a picture of a horned lark yet. I really want to. They're really unique-looking birds," she told Nikki. "Bright yellow throats, and these black-and-white striped faces. Greased lightning hairdos and a handlebar mustache."

Eric laughed and asked, "Have you been to Kennebunk Plains in late summer? Purple flowers everywhere."

"The northern blazing stars," Anna said with a smile. "I have."

"Your smile is so like your mother's." For a second, Eric looked stricken. Then, he sucked in a breath and grinned. "Did you know that they burn those plains on purpose? Prescribed burns, to keep the trees from taking over. The same way the Indians managed the great plains."

"As I understand it, most native peoples managed their environments pretty intensively. They just did it in a way that worked *with* nature rather than against it. I stayed with this group of scientists for a while, along the Amazon river. The botanists told me that basically the entire forest in that area is one massive garden, all of these food-bearing trees that people had planted centuries before."

"That's truly astonishing," Eric said with genuine amazement.

"It was the same here, with the American chestnut and the other mast trees... All of these phenomenal food forests... Have you read *The Overstory*?"

Eric shook his head and she continued.

"It's a novel, but it talks about how trees communicate with each other and take care of each other. In real life they do. They can warn each other if they're being attacked by bugs, and they can coordinate how much food to produce each year in order to control the animal population. Then, when they have a mast year, there's so much extra that it doesn't all get eaten and new trees can grow. Did you know that some forests keep their elders alive? They'll keep the root system alive underground, feeding it even after the tree falls. And when a massive tree finally does die, it gives everything it had back to its children."

Was she babbling? Anna glanced up. Eric was listening with rapt attention, and she looked back down at her plate.

"Amazing."

"I wish I could've seen them. Those forests of massive American chestnuts. But we were born too late. I feel like I've spent my whole life seeking out bits of nature that haven't been ruined yet."

"You're doing God's work," Eric said earnestly.

Anna looked at him. "Taking pictures?"

"Taking pictures." Eric nodded. "Your pictures make the animals come alive. They make people see why those places that they have left are worth protecting—expanding, even. That's why the nature conservancy hired you, isn't it?"

"Yes, um, I guess so." Anna nodded, struck dumb again by his passion for her work. She was glad when the rest of the meal passed in a haze of small talk and companionable silence as they tucked into the food in earnest.

"I wish I had some dessert to offer you, but I've been on something of a sweets fast. Just taking a break between Thanksgiving and Christmas."

"That's okay, Dad," Nikki said. "It's not like you were expecting us."

"Let's go sit in the living room, shall we?" He led the way and turned on all of the lights. With the room fully illuminated, Anna spotted something that she hadn't seen on her way in. An entire wall was devoted to three large photographs.

Her photographs.

The three images didn't work as a set. Even the frames were different. They were from three separate collections—different *decades* even. Each photograph showed a bird in flight. There was a picture of a Laysan albatross that she'd taken on Kauai. A resplendent quetzal in Guatemala. And a bluebird, here in Maine. That one was *old*...from her first exhibit, nearly thirty years ago.

Where in the world had he found it?

The sharp, bright pictures looked so out of place in this drab, cozy room. Anna felt close to tears again, and she turned away. She shot a glance toward Eric, who now stood in the corner, sorting through a large box that sat next to a record player.

"Did you know about this?" Anna whispered to Nikki.

"About what?"

Anna gestured sharply towards the photos.

Nikki frowned in confusion, and then gasped. "Are those *yours*?"

Anna nodded wordlessly.

"I saw them and thought they were great, but didn't put two and two together. He's had a lot of bird photos over the years." She pursed her lips and nodded slowly. "Now that I think about it, Beth *told* me that Dad had been asking her how to use eBay. He wouldn't tell her why. She figured it was for a Christmas present. Apparently she was wrong."

The record player kicked on and Nat King Cole's voice came softly through the room. Eric and Nikki settled onto the couch and Anna sat across from them, perched on the edge of a large recliner. They were quiet for a moment, sipping their drinks as Cole sang *Unforgettable*. Then Eric cleared his throat and leaned forward, bracing his arms on his knees.

"Do you have any questions for me, Anna? Anything you want to know? If you'd rather focus on the here and now or —" He faltered slightly and cleared his throat again. "The future, that's fine by me. But if there's anything you want to ask or... anything you'd like to say to me. I'm all ears."

Anna looked past him, checking in with Nikki. The younger woman shrugged and managed an encouraging smile as if to say, *"It's okay.* I'm *okay. Let it rip."*

"Did you love my mother?" Anna blurted. "Did she love you?"

Eric glanced at Nikki, who nodded and patted his arm. He leaned back with a sigh, letting the ancient couch embrace him.

"There's more than one kind of love," he said thoughtfully. "And Rose and I loved one another in the way you love someone you haven't lived a life with... Someone you haven't spent time in the trenches with. That puppy love, where everything is perfect. There's no compromising or arguing...no chilly silences or petty resentments that sneak in over the years. No one is snoring, or stealing the covers, or making snide comments because they're tired. We only got the very best of each other, the way you do when things are new."

He folded his hands on his lap, lips tipping into a fond smile.

"Your mother was so incredibly kind to me. She was bright and curious and beautiful. She listened to my silly stories, my hopes and dreams. She was the one I could turn to when I was low, someone who would tell me I wasn't failing as badly as I thought I was. And I think I was the same to her. She had her own troubles, some very dark days...we saw each other through.

He turned toward Nikki, smile fading as he continued. "A better man would have put that energy into his marriage, tried that much harder to be there for the mother of his children. Things were difficult then. Just after the twins were born, Wanda packed up and went to her mother's. That's when I started going to the library..." He bowed his head.

"I never knew that," Nikki said, shaking her head slowly. "Why didn't you tell us?"

"Because it doesn't matter," Eric said with a shrug. "That didn't give me license to be unfaithful. She came back, and then left again...it was never a 'forever' thing. I knew that after the first time. I'm not trying to put the blame for any of this on your mother. I would never. I'm just trying to give Anna some context as far as how it all happened."

He took a shuddering breath and then met Anna's gaze.

"I have my regrets. A lot of them, to be frank," he said quietly. "But Anna? You aren't one of them."

She swallowed hard past the lump in her throat and nodded.

She'd asked, and he'd answered. He didn't try to pretend he was a victim in all this, and he seemed to take ownership of his failings as a husband and father. That counted for something, in her book.

"I'll be right back," he said as he pushed himself to his feet.

He headed down the hallway, leaving her and Nikki alone in the living room.

"You okay?" Anna murmured, shooting a glance at Nikki.

Her sister nodded and raked one hand through her hair. "Yeah. It's actually good to get him talking about it. Other times, my siblings sort of stopped him. Cut him short, because they didn't want to hear it... but it's actually kind of a relief to hear the whole story. Like letting the last of the poison drain out."

Anna couldn't argue with that, and she nodded silently. Her thoughts and emotions were a jumbled mess, but search as she might, she couldn't find even a trace of the anger that had burned so hot when she'd first found out the truth.

She felt...free.

Eric stepped back into the room a moment later, offering Anna an envelope.

"Rose and I swore we would never contact each other, and we didn't. Except for a letter I got at my job one day, a few years later. Just this one letter."

Anna turned the envelope over, and sure enough, Eric's name and the address were written on the front in her mother's familiar scrawl. No return address.

She opened it, gut churning, and a picture fell out. A faded photograph of Anna as a toddler. Her vision blurred, and she blinked tears away to see a smiling baby with honey-brown curls and a red Christmas dress.

She unfolded the letter.

Eric,

I'll abide by our agreement after this, I swear. But I wanted you to have this.

Her name is Anna.

Isn't she beautiful? She is so full of life, such a little explorer. This girl would disappear into the woods without a backwards glance if I let her.

I may have broken my own heart, and Red's... I still lose sleep at night, thinking of the pain I caused him, the pain that we caused your family. I'll carry that guilt forever. But look at our girl. She's perfect. She's the most beautiful mistake I ever made, and I'll never regret making her. Not for a second.

I won't write again. I just wanted you to know that Anna is safe and happy and so, so loved. Red is crazy about her, and so am I.

I wish you and your family nothing but the best. Have a beautiful life, my friend.

Fondly,

Rose

A rush of love for both her mother and Pop crashed over her, and she had to take a second to catch her breath.

"Thank you," Anna finally croaked. She folded the letter and offered it to Eric, who shook his head.

"It's yours. I'll take the picture, though. If you don't mind."

Anna handed it over. "I have others... if you'd like."

Eric nodded rapidly and swiped a hand over his eyes.

"I would, yes. Please. Thank you." He took a seat across from Anna and looked her in the eye. "Thank you for coming. I am so grateful. I felt like my life would have ended on a comma if I had never met you." He paused and wet his lips. "Do you... think you'll stay awhile? I know you have a busy life. I get it. Just this... just this one visit was more than I ever dared to hope for. But if you can... if you do stay for a few days, maybe you'd like to go birding with me?"

A host of emotions still churned inside her. Painful threads of grief and guilt, all swamped by a torrent of love and gratitude. She swallowed the tears that threatened to take over again.

"I'd like that," she murmured. "I'd really like that."

6

LENA

LENA CHECKED her phone for the umpteenth time, waiting on a text from Nikki. Past eight at night, and still nothing.

Nikki's last text read, *Taking Anna to Dad's for dinner. I'll break the news to the AOE after. Wish us luck.*

Lena had sent back a four-leaf clover emoji and a single word.

LUCK.

Since then, radio silence. That was... probably a good sign?

She rubbed her aching neck and looked around at the strange part of purgatory in which she spent most of her days. Freddie's house was a piece of art unto itself. A bizarre one because, well, that was Freddie. He lived in an old button factory overlooking the Androscoggin River. The red brick exterior looked just the same as it always had. Freddie had gutted the interior, ripping out floors and walls. The main room took up half of the building. It was mostly empty, and what little furniture he did allow was all in shades of gray. Just like the concrete floors, and the steel pillars, and the walls. This was Freddie's main workspace, and he liked a blank slate.

The roof above Lena's head was the ceiling of the building, three stories up. She wore two wool sweaters, plus a hat and scarf, and she was *still* cold. One more month and this room would be intolerable. There would be space heaters and extension cords all over the place. It was almost too cold to work in here now, even though she was wearing fingerless gloves...not unlike the squatters who had been living here when Freddie bought the place.

Lena had dealt with them. She had coaxed them out, contacted local shelters, found housing for each and every one of the people who had been sleeping in the chill and gloom of the abandoned factory. Some had disappeared, unwilling to abide by the shelters' rules. Others had gotten back on their feet. One sent her a Christmas card every year from a farmhouse in New Hampshire.

After that, Lena had overseen the renovations. Freddie had consulted with the architects, come up with the grand plan, but bringing it to fruition? It had been on her. All of the details, all of the follow through. Always. She had taken on a job as Freddie's assistant over a decade ago, and now she managed pretty much every aspect of his life. Everything that Freddie couldn't be bothered to see to himself. So basically, everything but his art. Hell, she even did the tedious parts of that.

Case in point, here she was, well after hours, sitting on a throw rug over a cold, concrete floor of an abandoned button factory, cutting the tips off of matchsticks for Freddie's next project.

How had he talked her into this nonsense?

She stood up and stretched her aching back. She was getting too old for late nights in this oversized nightmare of a living room. Freddie was cozy in his third-floor bedroom right now, leaving her to do the grunt work. Lena nudged a tower of matchboxes with her toe and watched it tumble.

A flash of color caught her eye, and she let it draw her across the cavernous room. She walked up the stairs to the open loft space that held the dining area and kitchen. Lena had begged Freddie to reconsider the second-floor kitchen, but hey. He wasn't the one who had to carry the groceries up here, after all.

She stood in front of her favorite painting and sighed.

This was why she put up with him. The jerk was a genius. The piece in front of her was twenty-five square feet, a riot of color that sang out from the flat gray concrete wall. It looked like nothing at first glance, just another abstract, albeit a visually arresting one. But then, the longer you looked, the more you saw. It was several things all at once. A sunset over the river, a sunrise over the ocean. Stare a minute longer, and the shapes that you'd taken for trees along the riverbank or boats on the water morphed into a crowd of people.

He'd titled it *Fluidity*, and it was a masterpiece.

For all of his tantrums, all of the self-inflicted drama and theatrics, Freddie was a genius.

Sometimes.

More often than not, Frederick swung hard and missed grandly. The endless tedium of the matchsticks for this three-dimensional piece would probably be for naught. There was a fair chance that Freddie would kick the thing to pieces before he'd even finished it.

When he was truly inspired, there was no stopping him.

He had painted it in front of her in less than a week, hardly pausing to eat or sleep. But the rest of the time, when he tried to force that inspiration? They wound up with painfully bad pieces. Lena's mind flashed back to one in particular, called "*Rubber Duckies, Only Sadder*", and she winced.

Yup. Old Freddie was a mixed bag.

Weren't they all, though?

When she headed back down the stairs, she found her boss sitting in her former spot, cross-legged amongst tens of thousands of matchsticks, super-gluing them together one at a time. Overgrown, bleached-blond hair hung in front of his eyes. Lena had tried to tell him that his current hairdo made him look like a mad scientist, but Freddie had taken that as a compliment.

"Were you looking for food?" he asked without looking up. "There's no food."

"Are you hungry?" Lena asked patiently.

"Yes. Do you want to order in Chinese?"

"Sure."

"Add an egg roll. I have the calories to spare, seeing as how I didn't eat breakfast."

The bakery had been out of chocolate croissants, and he had turned his nose up at the bear claw Lena had brought instead. "Lovely of you to remind me," she said as she retrieved her phone from amongst the matchsticks. She ordered their usual favorites, plus some egg rolls. She hung up, and her boss shot her a disgruntled glance.

"*What?*" she demanded. "What now?"

"Pickup would have been faster," he said with an indignant sniff.

"Can you give it a rest?" Lena crossed to the gray couch

that stood in the middle of the gray room and sat down. "I'm in the middle of some major family drama over here."

"Family drama, you say?"

Interest piqued, Freddie abandoned his tiny wall and crossed to where Lena sat. He poured them each a glass of absinthe from the wheeled drink cart that stood near the couch. Lena topped hers off with water before taking a sip. Even watered down, the drink was *strong*. Alcoholic, bitter green licorice. Freddie drank his neat, like a lunatic. The man could hold his liquor.

He curled up on the couch and gave her his full attention, wide gray eyes and an eager smile.

"Spill it, sister."

"Anna's in town."

"The long-lost sister?" Freddie's eyebrows rose. "Last I heard, she wanted nothing to do with any of you. This is getting juicy."

"Juicy like a bad telenovela. I'm ready to change the channel."

"You don't like her?"

"I don't *not* like her." Lena frowned. "I don't even know her. I just wish we could skip over the collective meltdown that's coming. The twins don't even know that Anna's in town. She's having dinner with Dad tonight and I have no idea how it's going. I just want to fast forward to the end part, where Jack and Gayle have settled into a grudging acceptance."

"You dream too small." Freddie regarded her with a sardonic smile.

Little did he know.

"Thanks, Freddie," she said with an acidic smile.

Her boss's eyes narrowed at her use of the nickname, and he stalked back over to his work in progress. Lena took another sip of her absinthe and winced, wishing that Freddie had something normal to drink in this infernal place. Her phone buzzed and she picked it up, expecting Nikki. Owen's name flashed across the screen, along with his picture. Well, a picture of Owen at thirteen, with braces and a Pink Floyd shirt. It helped Lena keep things in perspective.

"Hi, Owen," she answered.

"Hey there, love," Owen said cheerfully.

Damn him for making her heart flutter without even trying. *He calls his baby sister the same dang thing,* she scolded herself.

"I just finished working," he was saying. "Wanna grab a burger at Gayle's?"

Lena and Owen met up at her sister's pub at least once a week to catch up and decompress. Their friend Jenna was working tonight, too. She always joined them at the end of her shift. Lena wanted nothing more than to kick back at The Milky Thistle with a fat cheeseburger and one of Gayle's tart and tasty cocktails. But even if she could get away from work, she wasn't ready to look Gayle in the face.

"I can't," Lena mumbled. "I'm working late."

"It's past time you quit that job." That intoxicating brogue of his made Lena want to agree with anything he said, and the absinthe wasn't helping. She set the glass down. The things that Owen had talked her into in their teenage years... He had nicked his dad's keys, more than once, to take her to Sebago Lake to watch the sunrise. It sounded romantic, and it might have been, but it was never just the two of them. There had always been other people along on their adventures, friends who had moved away and fallen out of contact over the years. It was just the two of them, now, though. A fact he seemed oblivious to.

"Lena?" he said when she didn't answer. "Are you okay?"

"I'm still having a rough day," she admitted softly.

"Do you want me to come get you? I'll kidnap you. What's he going to do, stop me? I can take Freddie in a bare-knuckle brawl, you know I can."

"Ha ha."

"We can meet up when you're done," he offered in a more serious tone. "Talk it over?"

"No. I appreciate the offer, Owen, but when I'm done here I just need to go home and sleep."

Also, if I see your stupid, beautiful face tonight, I'm going to cry.

She cleared her throat. "Coffee and a bite early tomorrow morning, maybe?"

"I'll hold you to that," he threatened cheerfully. "Meet me at Sadie's at eight. I'll buy you a whole box of macarons, and I promise not to crush them this time."

"Deal," she said, and hung up.

A hollow banging sound echoed through the room – Freddie had spurned Lena's suggestion of a doorbell in favor of a huge, old-fashioned knocker in the shape of a dragon hung on the front door – and Lena went to fetch their dinner. She paid with one of Freddie's credit cards, giving the delivery girl a hefty tip, and then laid out their meal on the hideous steel coffee table.

"Come eat before it gets cold."

Freddie looked up, blinking himself out of a daze. That was a good sign. Maybe this tedious matchbox-million project would turn into something interesting after all. Lena grabbed the iPad she used for work and settled onto the couch with a box of fried rice.

"We'll keep working on this tomorrow morning."

"All right, but don't forget, you're meeting Sandra Hurst for lunch tomorrow," she told him between bites.

He looked up from the meal he was arranging on a delicate glass plate. It was one of Owen's decorative pieces, and Freddie seemed to find perverse pleasure in eating off of it.

"Who in the seventh circle of hell is Sandra Hurst?" he demanded.

"She runs the gallery on Fifth."

"Oh. Her." He let out a disgruntled sigh.

"Yes, her. If you want to get last year's paintings out of storage, you'll play nice."

"I do not enjoy playing nice."

"I know, but you're good at it. If you want to maintain your finances and retain my services, you'll do it more often," she continued crossly.

"Mercenary wench," he said through a mouthful of tofu.

"After that, you have dinner with Manuel and then drinks with the Randazzo sisters. The next day is the twenty-eighth—"

"November twenty-eighth?" he interrupted, cheeks going pale. "Crap. That's my mother's birthday. I totally forgot!"

She nodded and plucked up a piece of broccoli. "But I didn't. You're treating her and her friends to a dinner of Maine lobster, delivered with all the fixings, along with two dozen peach roses and a hand-written card."

"You wrote a card?"

"*You* wrote the card," she said, leveling him with a steely glare. "I dictated it to you two weeks ago."

He squinted and then nodded. "Yeah...yeah, that sounds vaguely familiar."

Lena rolled her eyes and took another bite of beef fried rice. Lord give her patience to deal with this man. Her phone buzzed and she picked it up, hoping again for Nikki.

Gayle's name flashed across the screen, along with a deceptively cheerful picture of a much younger Gayle with her two kids. Lena ignored the first call...and the second, thirty seconds later. But when she received a voicemail notification, she blew out a sigh and pressed play, just in case it was an emergency or something.

Gayle's voice screeched into her ear, and Lena immediately held the phone at arm's length. There were a few more seconds of incoherent shouting, and then her words became crystal clear.

"She's here. Do you understand what I'm telling you? She's. Here. Nikki brought Anna to Dad's house, and I'm going to freaking kill *her."*

Annnnd, so much for her day improving...

7

GAYLE

NINE ON A WEEKNIGHT and The Milky Thistle was hopping. This place was Gayle's second home, her third child. She had opened the bar after her daughter Maddy went off to college and her son Reid was a high school junior who was way too cool to hang out with his mom... but still quietly proud that she had opened her own "supercool, swanky bar". The adjectives were all his, from the day he had come to see the almost-finished space. The memory still made Gayle smile.

It had been a labor of love. She had decided on every detail of the bar's decor, from the wooden floors to the open shelving. Antique bottles lined the top shelves and everyday options stood where she could reach them. The furniture was all made of reclaimed wood, most of it from the same local barn. Maddy had painted the ceiling during her first summer home from college, just before the grand opening. It was twilight blue, dotted with constellations of tiny stars. Bright greens and purples colored the corners of the room, Maddy's gorgeous interpretation of the northern lights that they had seen in Alaska the year before. Reid had strung LED lights down the center of each ribbon of paint so that they shone vibrant colors.

With both of her children grown and gone, Gayle spent just as much time at The Milky Thistle now as she had in those uncertain early days. It had been touch and go for a few years before she finally turned a profit. These days, business was thriving and the work felt comfortable but still satisfying. She could make any of the cocktails with her eyes closed, and her attention was focused on the people around her. Her employees and regulars made the bar an easy, inviting place — and the constant flow of tourists kept things interesting, especially this time of year. There was always a final rush of people before the holidays. After that, things got quiet. But the regulars could always be trusted to come in for a bite to eat, sample Gayle's latest creations, and stick around to chat.

One of those regulars, a longtimer named Anthony, claimed a seat at the bar. He was an amiable guy, Nikki's age, with bright blue eyes and a receding hairline. His kids were in middle school; they lived a few towns over with their mom and stayed with him most weekends.

Weeknights he usually had dinner at The Milky Thistle.

"Do you still have that maple wine?" he asked without preamble.

"Hello, Anthony," Gayle said without looking up from the drink she was making. "Nice to see you, Anthony. How's the family, *Anthony*?" she asked pointedly.

"Hello, Gayle," he said with a grin. "Nice to see you, Gayle. The family's fine, thank you."

"There. Was that so hard?"

"Nowhere else in town do I have to greet them as if I showed up to someone's house for dinner."

"And yet you keep coming here," Gayle said cheerfully. She set the finished drink on a tray with its fellows, and a server whisked it away to one of the community tables.

"Only because Jimmy makes the best burgers in town," he muttered, shooting her a mock-scowl.

"I'll tell him you said so when I put your order in."

"I'll take a bacon barbecue burger with fries."

"Sounds good. We don't have any more of the blackfeather maple wine, but I do have a new maple mead that you're going to love." Gayle was already pouring him a glass. "I've outdone myself with this one. You're the first to taste it, besides me and Jo. I used mostly maple syrup, with some orange blossom honey."

Anthony took a sip and his eyes widened. "You're a genius."

"I know it," said Gayle with a smile. Down the bar, a pair of new faces ordered two Saints and Strangers cocktails and she got to work as Anthony continued chatting with her.

"You get any holiday shopping done?" he asked idly as he glanced over the specials menu.

"Not a lick," she replied as she filled two shakers with ice. "I will start next week and most of it will be online. How about you?"

"A little. And the kids are already on me about putting up a tree, so we'll be doing that this weekend." He went quiet for a moment and then brightened. "I was glad to see Nikki's back in town. It's been a while, and I've been missing the Sunday stew specials over at the Lighthouse Inn. Plus,

Cherry Blossom Point isn't quite the same without its full complement of Merrills," he added with a chuckle.

His words finally registered and her hand twitched, causing cranberry juice to miss its mark, creating a blood-red pool on the countertop.

Gayle cleared her throat and moved to mop it up. "Nikki is back?"

Anthony frowned and nodded cautiously. "Yeah…I drove past your dad's place on my way home from work a couple hours ago. Nikki was walking in with a tray of food."

Gayle regarded him with narrowed eyes as she shook the cocktails, trying to ignore the warning bells blaring in her head.

Why would her sister not have told her she was back in town?

"You're sure it was her?"

"I spent most of my school career staring at the back of Nikki's head, cursing the fact that Moretti comes after Merrill on every roster. I had to lean around those curls for years to try and see the board. Yes, I'm sure…her and another woman, actually."

Gayle set down her cocktail shaker as blood rushed to her ears.

"W-what did she look like?"

"Curly hair," Anthony said, eyes narrowed in thought. "A bit lighter than Nikki's. Not Beth, she was taller and much older. I'm guessing mid-forties?"

Anna.

There was no doubt in her mind.

"What's wrong?" he asked, but she ignored him.

"Hey, Jo?" she called over to her second-in-command,

who stood chatting with tourists at the far end of the bar. "I need to take ten."

Jo-anne gave her a quizzical frown. Not at the request, Gayle knew, but probably at the look on her face. Because if she looked anything like she felt, it was something akin to getting smacked in the face with an eel.

"A-yup," she said. "Everything okay?"

Gayle nodded and scurried into the kitchen, paused to tell Jimmy to send out a burger for Anthony, and then headed out the back door. The fire escape was frigid, exposed to the wind that rushed through the back alley, but at least no one else came out here. Gayle pulled her phone from her pocket and paused before calling Jack.

Straight to voicemail.

Gayle hung up and took a deep breath... or tried to, but kept getting that same feeling of her diaphragm sticking to her ribs. Jack was going to lose his mind when he found out. She needed to pull herself together.

She could call Nikki first. Make sure her hunch was right...

No. It was Anna. It had to be. She could feel it in her bones.

She held her phone for a long moment and then found herself pressing Lena's name, waiting through the rings.

Nothing. Gayle hung up and tried a second time.

Voicemail. Again. Lena's voice was in her ear, breezy and blasé. Then a shrill beep.

"Why do you never answer your phone?" Gayle demanded. She thought of Lena's behavior that morning and her temper flared. "When it's anyone but me, you'll pick up, but me you won't even look me in the eye. What is *with* you lately? This is an emergency." She took a breath and tried to keep it slow and concise. "She's here. Do you understand what I'm telling you? She's. Here. Nikki brought Anna to Dad's house, and I'm going to freaking kill her."

Her own voice bounced back at her from the brick walls all around. She hung up and shoved her phone back in her pocket, at a loss as to what to do with all her rage. How could Nikki do this to her? To *them*. It was a slap to their mother's face, didn't she realize that? And to take this choice away from her, from all of them...

She spun on her heel and stomped back through the kitchen, grabbing Anthony's plate just as one of the cooks added the last drizzle of barbecue sauce. She set it on the bar without pause or comment and stalked over to the games corner, which was in its usual state of disarray.

Why did no one clean up after themselves? Why did it always fall on her?

Gayle was too angry to stand and chat with guests like nothing was wrong, but she could do something useful and organize this infernal games cabinet.

It had stood in her house once. For years, it had held all of her kids' favorite games. From the shoots-and-ladders years all the way up through high school. She had moved it to the restaurant after Reid left for college so patrons could play on slower nights when they wanted to unwind. It had accumulated more games over the years until it was full to bursting. All the classics mixed together with hipster games that she didn't even know how to play. The cards on the coffee table had intricate illustrations: flowers and dragons, hideous creatures and swirls of color. Gayle stacked them neatly and put them into a wooden box marked Magic the

Gathering and then swept a mess of checkers pieces into their own tattered cardboard box.

She pulled out her phone and glanced at the screen.

Nothing.

She put it away and began to scrub at the stained surface of a nearby table.

A raucous shout of glee sounded from across the room, and Gayle looked up. Jo-anne "Big Jo" Patreski stood with a grin on her face and her hand held out. Four young guys were paying up. A storm of anxieties swirled in Gayle's head, and yet she couldn't help but grin at her friend.

Jo was nearly six feet tall, with wiry gray hair that she made no effort to tame. With her square face, rough hands, and lumberjack body, Jo looked like she should be working on the docks or reeling in an 800-pound tuna, but she actually made the most delicately flavored cocktails in Cherry Blossom Point. That didn't stop her from using her size and wits to hustle tourists—and a few tragically stubborn townies—into arm wrestling her for cash.

"Better luck next time, boys." Jo turned and walked over to Gayle, stuffing the cash into her bra as she crossed the room. "You scrub that any harder," she warned, "and you're going to wear off that fresh layer of polyurethane I just applied."

Gayle didn't answer, and Jo sat across from her on the leather couch.

"What's going on, boss?"

"Anna's in town," Gayle muttered through gritted teeth as she scrubbed.

Jo winced and laid one huge hand over hers, forcing Gayle to release the towel she was abusing.

"Your *sister* Anna?"

"Our *half*-sister that Nikki went looking for, yes. Apparently, Nikki took her to our father's house for dinner. Without asking or even telling the rest of us. I'm livid."

Jo squeezed Gayle's hand and stood.

"I'm on the bar, and I can close up. You go home."

"What?" Gayle frowned up at her friend. "No, I'm fine to stay."

"You're not," Jo shot back, crossing her arms over her barrel chest. "If you want to hash this out over breakfast tomorrow, I'm there. But for now, we've got a bar to run and you're no use to anyone. Poor Anthony thinks he offended you."

She muttered a curse. "I'll go apologize."

"He's fine," Jo said firmly. "He doesn't need an apology, but the next guy might. So you go home and get your head together."

She was right. Gayle couldn't tend to customers tonight. She couldn't even remember what she had said in her voicemail to Lena. She had worked too long and hard on this place to lose even one customer due to Nikki's selfishness.

"Okay." She stood and untied the black cotton apron that she wore. "I'll be in tomorrow early for inventory, though."

Jo gave her a pat on the back. "I'll make my hamburger-bun French toast for us."

Gayle pulled Jo in for a quick hug. What would she do without this woman? She hoped she'd never have to find out. Jo had been Gayle's dearest friend for over twenty years, ever since their kids were babies. Jo had raised one child on her own, a son who was right between Maddy and Reid in age.

He had gone to Portland for college and then moved home to Cherry Blossom Point.

"Thank you, Jo."

Gayle drove home on autopilot. One minute she was opening the door to her Lexus, and the next minute she was sitting in front of her house, with zero recollection of the ride. That couldn't be safe.

Her husband's car was in the driveway, and Gayle glanced at the clock radio in surprise. Ten at night and Rex was already home? Strange. He rarely came home before she did, and Gayle usually got home after midnight. Of course, she could sleep in. She wondered how he made do with so little rest. But he had always been that way. He had been such a trooper in the early days, up with the babies just as much as she was, even though he had work the next day.

Gayle shook her head and sighed.

Where had *that* Rex gone? The partner. The friend. The confidant. Because he certainly didn't live here anymore.

She shoved the thought aside and headed into the house. When Gayle walked into the living room, she found him on the couch watching TV. He greeted her with a glance and a vague smile, and she couldn't help but think how handsome he was.

Golden hair that held its color years after Gayle began to cover her gray with boxes of dye. His hazel eyes changed with the light. The effect that smile had had on her once...

These days, though, she noted his good looks with a strange sort of detachment. Like a statue that had been sitting in her home for years, she was aware of his features, but they no longer stirred any of the emotion they once had.

She tugged her phone from her pocket and spared the screen a quick glance.

Still nothing.

Jack hadn't called. Lena hadn't called. Nikki hadn't called...not that Gayle had much hope on that last front.

She tossed the cell onto a side table and plopped onto the opposite end of the couch from her husband.

She probably shouldn't even try...

"Nikki's back in town."

"Oh yeah?" Rex muttered without looking up.

"She brought Anna with her. From Bluebird Bay..."

He didn't react, not even a little.

"She brought our half-sister, the product of my father's affair, back with her to our home town," she pressed, her blood pressure rising with every word. "She took her to Dad's house without even talking to us."

Rex glanced at her and then back to the TV. "Might not be such a bad idea. Rip off the band-aid."

A wave of disgust for this complacent brick of a man rolled over her, but it faded almost immediately, morphing into a bone-deep exhaustion.

"I'm going to take a shower and go to bed."

Rex replied with a non-committal grunt, and Gayle walked away.

The hallway that led from the living room to her bedroom was lined with pictures from happier times. As she slowly made the trek, scanning the images, she realized with a start that she could almost see Rex pulling away like in a movie.

In their wedding photo, Rex stood half next to her and half behind her. Both of his arms were wrapped around her waist. They were so young, grinning like fools. She couldn't even remember what it felt like to be held that tightly, not really. In each of the photos that marked the passing of the years, Rex stood a little further away. In one picture taken just before Gayle's baby shower, he stood with one arm around her waist and a photo-smile plastered on his face. In the others, there was a baby between them, or two children. In most of the later pictures, it was just Gayle and the kids on summer trips that they had taken without him. He was always too busy with work to join them.

Or so he claimed.

The hallway ended with two more wedding photos. Their daughter Maddy had gotten married three years ago, and Reid had finally married his college sweetheart this past summer.

At least she had them. And who knew? Maybe she even had grandchildren to look forward to. Maddy had hinted that they were trying. Wouldn't that be lovely...

She turned away, and a picture on the opposite wall caught her eye. A family photo taken a few years before her mom had passed away. Tears burned Gayle's eyes and she blinked them away.

Nope. Not now. The last thing she needed to be thinking about right now was her mother, because that would make her think about Nikki, and that would make her think about—

She cut off that train of thought with a ruthless snip as she headed through the master bedroom and straight into her bathroom. Maybe a nice, long, hot bath—

She frowned as she caught sight of Rex's suit jacket hanging from the bathroom door. It reeked of lilacs, so much so that Gayle nearly gagged as she brushed past it. Simmering fury bubbled over as she grabbed the jacket, stalked across the room, and threw it down the hall.

"I told you to stop using my bathroom!" she shouted.

"The water pressure in the hall shower sucks," he called back.

"So fix it!" Gayle went back into her room and slammed the door behind her, wishing like hell she could open it and slam it again just because it felt good, but not wanting to give him the satisfaction. Wouldn't he have a lovely time complaining about her to his mistress, making her out to be the bad guy.

Idiot.

She was pretty sure Rex still thought his affair was the best kept secret in Cherry Blossom Point. Little did he know that she never confronted him or asked about it because she didn't *want* to know. She didn't want to hear his confession or his lies. So long as he stayed out of her bed and in the spare room, that was good enough for her.

Gayle went to the bathroom sink and scrubbed the cloying smell of lilac from her hands.

She might look like the village idiot who didn't know her husband was cheating, but she'd be damned if she would be the sucker who didn't know that her father's bastard child had blown into town on top of it. A woman could only take so much.

It was time she made Nikki face the music and let her know how things were going to be from now on.

She snatched up the bedroom phone and dialed.

8

LENA

Lena checked her watch as she sat in her car across the street from Sadie's place, scanning the other cars on the street. Eight AM, and no sign of her sister's Lexus. Although, there were those spots around back...

But Gayle usually spent Wednesday morning at The Milky Thistle, accepting deliveries and restocking the shelves. She wouldn't be at the cafe this morning.

Coward.

She got out of her car, leaving her sunglasses on. She pulled the hood of her jacket up against the biting cold of the early December morning and kept it up as she stepped inside the cafe and got into line.

Not because she was scared. She just ran cold. This was normal. Toooootally normal.

Lena jumped at a sudden tap on her shoulder, but it was only Owen.

"I already ordered," he said. "For the both of us. I got our favorite table in the corner."

"Oh. Thanks. Sorry. I didn't see you."

Owen cocked one eyebrow and grinned. "No, you wouldn't have. Incognito today, are we?" He placed one hand on the small of her back and ushered her away from the long line.

Lena laughed self-consciously and removed her sunglasses. There were breakfast bagels waiting – one topped with lox and onions, the other with Sadie's lucious feta scrambled eggs. Owen had switched two halves so that both plates had one of each kind.

"I haven't forgotten your macarons." Owen gestured to a white box as he sat down. "But I thought you should start your day with some real sustenance."

"Thank you." Lena pushed her hood back, freeing her ungovernable curls. "We are going to be continuing our work on this crazy matchstick project at Freddie's place, so I'll need the fuel to keep me from dying of boredom."

"Why the disguise?" he asked between sips of coffee.

"Just hoping to avoid a public confrontation is all."

"Oh?" Owen smiled gently, dark blue eyes intent on her face.

"Gayle called and left a message last night, shrieking like a banshee." She shook her head and took a bite of her food. Fragrant basil and pillowy eggs on a fresh, chewy bagel. On top of being a great person and an amazing mother to Jack's son, Wyatt, Sadie was a genius. Jack was a fool for letting her go.

"Do you know what a banshee is, for real?" Owen asked quizzically.

"What?" Lena stared at him blankly. "They're, um, the eagle ladies who pluck soldiers off the battlefield, I think?"

"That's harpies you're thinking of, darling," he said, his

lips hitching into a crooked grin. "The banshee is a fairy woman. Her cries are mournful beyond any other sound on this earth — or so my granny used to tell me. According to the old folks, the wailing of a banshee foretells a death in the family."

Lena felt the blood drain from her face. "Geez, don't say that. I already lost my mom. No more deaths in this family, not for a long time."

"*You* said it. And it was only your sister you were talking about, not the real thing. My granny wouldn't even let us speak the word. She said she had heard the noise as a child when her mother was ill, the night before she died."

For a fraction of a heartbeat, Lena was a small girl in Ireland, hiding beneath the covers as her mother sickened and a keening woman wailed outside. She blinked, and she was back in Sadie's bright and bustling cafe, sharing a phenomenal breakfast with her oldest friend.

It put things in perspective.

"Sorry, love," Owen said with a quick squeeze of her hand, and Lena scolded her foolish heart for doing a somersault. "The word brought me back, and I could hear my grandmother's voice as clear as I hear your own. But to my point, I don't think Gayle was wailing like a banshee. She was more shrieking like a harpy. So what was she shrieking about this time?"

"Anna. She found out that she's in town...before Nikki got around to telling her about it."

Owen winced and leaned back in his chair. "Nikki knows there are no secrets in Cherry Blossom Point," he said with a cheeky smile.

Lena shrugged and took another bite of her bagel. He was

right. She should have told Gayle the moment Anna came to town. In fact, she should have told all of them about it *before* Anna came to town. But there was nothing to be done about that now. Might as well use this stay of execution wisely and enjoy her morning. Once the Axis struck, things were going to be miserable for the near future.

"You know, if you need reinforcements," Owen said around a bite of food, "I'm always around."

Lena shook her head and smiled. "I'll manage." No point in dragging Owen into the line of fire with her. "But let's talk about something less depressing. How's *your* sister doing?"

Owen accepted her clumsy change of topic without batting an eye.

"Moving to Massachusetts as we speak. She's got the kids in the car and Jerry's driving a rental truck containing their every worldly possession."

Lena stared at him in shock, chewing a salty bite of smoked salmon. She swallowed and said, "How have I not heard about this? I thought Gemma loved it in Colorado." Like Gayle's kids, Gemma had left for college and never moved home again. She'd lived in Denver for the past twenty years. This was a huge move for her and her family.

"She did. She does. But they couldn't afford it anymore. You know that they've been in the same two-bedroom condo for thirteen years? The kids were sharing a room. Fine when they were wee lads, but now that they're going to be teens soon, not so much."

"I didn't know they were having financial issues."

He nodded. "Then Jerry got laid off, and they couldn't even afford that place anymore."

"That's terrible."

"Save your pity." Owen laughed. "He's a new man. That job was killing him."

She knew the feeling.

"Besides, Gemma's making enough money working remotely to support them in fine fashion somewhere less ridiculous. I think it'll be good for them."

"Two decades in Colorado and I never made it out there to visit her," Lena said mournfully. Owen had invited her to go along with him, more than once. Lena loved Gemma. But it had always been something. Plans with an ex or, more often, work...

"Well, now we'll just have to visit them in Mass. It's a really pretty area. Remember that time I went to Mass for a few months? I even worked in Boston for a while..."

"Of course I remember." In fact, she'd been gutted thinking he'd never move back to Maine. "You were still doing tattoos then."

He held out his arm and pointed to one of her favorites, a sun radiating ombre waves of light. "Got this one at a little shop in Roxbury."

Without thought, she reached out and traced the circle with her fingertip and then stopped short, snatching her hand away.

Owen's ocean eyes held hers for a long moment. "I'm not going to bite, love."

Her throat stuck together and her pulse hitched.

"Yes, well, that's good," she replied primly.

Owen's crooked grin flashed for just an instant before it disappeared again.

"Anyway, point is, Gemma will be fine," he said as he pulled his arm back and settled against his chair. "I tried to convince her to come home to Maine, but she wouldn't hear of it. Her best friend moved to Cape Cod a year ago, and their kids grew up together. Ten and twelve are tricky ages for a move, but the boys are excited to be near those friends again."

"I'm sorry they won't be moving here," Lena said. "I know how much you love your nephews." About as much as Lena loved her own nieces and nephews, which was gobs. It had been twenty years, and not a day passed that she didn't think about the one she'd lost...

She pushed the painful memories aside and continued.

"But at least she'll be driving distance now."

"That's the good part. And they're coming here for Christmas," he said brightly. "Gemma's not putting them into school right away; they're going to take a couple weeks to get settled, and then they're going to spend three weeks out here."

"Oh good!" Lena finished her bagel and opened the box of macarons that sat waiting. Owen had gotten her three of everything, and she couldn't decide which to try.

"I can't wait to take the kids snowboarding. I'm going to take them to that indoor skating bowl too, the one with the climbing wall and the trampolines. I got them new boards for Christmas, snow *and* skate."

"Wow! They're going to have a blast." Lena drank the last sip of her coffee. "Speaking of Christmas, I meant to tell you...I loved your display. Those plates are so beautiful, Owen."

He smiled bashfully and grabbed a chocolate macaron. "They're too fancy to eat off of. I doubt they'll sell. I think I'm going back to functional items after this. I'll keep the ombre but make things people can actually use. Solid stuff. Functional art."

"Art doesn't have to be useful, Owen. Those plates are stunning. I want to buy the poppy-colored one and hang it by my front door."

"Don't insult me," Owen shot back. "*Buy* a plate. As if I'd let Lena Merrill pay me for a piece of glass. I'll give it to you, and be glad to get rid of it."

"Don't talk like that."

"I don't care about any of it, truly. I just like *making* them. That's the buzz for me. Once they're done, I'm ready to move on to something new."

Sort of like the women you date, she almost replied, only she was afraid a note of bitterness might creep in. Instead, she settled on, "You're impossible."

Owen grinned and swiped another macaron. "This is news to you?"

"Not at all." Lena looked over her options and chose a sunshine-yellow macaron. The delicate shell crumpled in her mouth, lemon-scented air and lucious vanilla cream. "How about the ornaments?"

"I'm rather proud of those," Owen admitted. "No more spots and blobs of color. Just elegant swirls and ombre."

"Gorgeous. So are all of your candlesticks."

He made a funny little gesture, like doffing a hat. "Here's hoping it goes well enough to get me through to the next holiday shopping season. I want to pull in a few more galleries next year. The official opening at Sheree's is this Saturday night, and I'm dreading it, if I'm honest. Be my date so I don't have to face it alone?"

Lena's cheeks flushed and she looked down under the

pretext of choosing another macaron. He didn't mean anything by it. It was just a word for his plus one.

Companion.

Chum.

"Don't make me beg."

"Of course I'll come." She popped another macaron in her mouth, and a mix of orange, cranberry, and cinnamon hit her all at once, like a Christmas flavor explosion.

"Sadie!" she called across the crowd.

Her former sister-in-law looked up with a start.

"The cranberry is the most delicious thing I've ever tasted in my life!"

Sadie thanked her with a laugh and turned back to the customers in front of her. "With Lena around, who needs advertising?"

"She's swamped, so I'm going to get my own refill. You want more coffee?" she asked Owen as she stood.

He handed her his empty cup, and she headed to the counter and helped herself to the coffee pot.

"Too good to stand in line like the rest of us?" teased a vaguely familiar voice. Lena glanced over and saw a man that she had met a few times before, a friend of Freddie's. *What the heck was his name again?*

Greg...no...Guy? No...

"Just helping out," she said with a smile, hoping it didn't come up. "They're mobbed today."

"It's been too long," the man said.

"Frederick's going through a reclusive phase."

"The muse needs time and attention, just like any lady." He smiled at her, flashing perfect white teeth. Was he flirting with her?

She took stock of his perfectly tailored suit and no-strand-out-of-place hair. He was attractive, in a fancy kind of way, but she felt no spark when she looked at him. Still, she was flattered. She had given the first half of her thirties to a relationship that had gone absolutely nowhere, and the second half of it, into her forties, to Freddie, so even a half-hearted coffee-shop pick-up was a nice little boost to her ego.

"I've got to get back to my friend, but I definitely recommend the cranberry macarons," Lena said with a smile, moving away.

"Lena, wait." He fished in his pocket and pulled out a card. *Guillermo*, it said. No surname. Just *Guillermo* and a phone number. "Call me sometime. Maybe we can get dinner."

"Thanks." Lena pocketed the card, not wanting to wound his pride with a flat, "*No thank you.*" "Good to see you."

She walked back to the table and set down the coffee mugs to find Owen mowing through her macarons.

"New admirer, then?" he asked through a mouthful of chocolate.

"Can you blame him?" Lena joked, gesturing to her oversized hoodie and wild hair. "I mean, look at me. I look like I just escaped Azkaban."

He swallowed. "I'm looking, Lena."

Owen's tone was strangely serious and she had to resist the urge to check her reflection in the window beside her. Was she really *that* much of a mess? She frowned and grabbed a pistachio macaron.

"I'm not sure which is better. The cranberry or the pistachio." Inspired, she put one on top of the other and took a bite.

Ambrosia.

"Man, you should try this."

"Don't you think he's a little short for you?"

Lena gave him a quizzical frown. "What?"

"Fancy suit guy," Owen continued with a nonchalant shrug. "He's short."

A chuckle escaped her as she caught his drift. "I'm not exactly tall and willowy myself, now, am I?"

Before Owen could reply, her phone buzzed. Lena looked down and instantly wished she hadn't.

Mandatory family meeting. 12pm at the bar.

Lena sighed and let out a groan.

"Let me guess," Owen quipped. "The governor called. You've been pardoned and the town can rejoice."

"No." She gave him a rueful smile and showed him the text. "The exact opposite, in fact. I'm a dead man walking."

"You've got to appreciate the *cojones* on that one," Owen said almost reverently as he read the text.

"I should skip the meeting and go get a pedicure instead." Then, she shook her head. "But what's the point? I'd just be putting off the inevitable."

"Do you want me to come with you? I can wait downstairs in the getaway car. First sign of a harpy and we're out of there."

"Thank you, but no. I can handle her."

"Course you can," he said in an exaggerated, posh British accent. "Stiff upper lip, love."

"Thank you for breakfast, but I've got to run." The box of macarons was half full. She closed it and picked it up. "These might just get me through the day with my sanity intact."

"Cheers to that." Owen raised his mug in a toast and then

finished his coffee. "I'll walk you out."

Once they'd said their goodbyes and Lena was behind the wheel with her seatbelt fastened, she dialed Nikki and set the call to speakerphone.

"Hey, Lena." Her sister picked up on the first ring. "I meant to call you last night, but we stayed at Dad's house later than I thought."

A bolt of relief shot through her. "It went well, then?"

"Yeah, it did. It was a lot, but it was good. He wants to take her birding."

"Wow." Their older siblings were going to lose their ever-loving mind. Birding was something their dad had tried to get them all into when they were younger, and only Jack had been interested. Once he heard Anna was in town, her brother might just wind up taking one of his famous treks into the wilderness and never come back.

"So... did you see the text from Gayle?" Lena asked, not bothering to beat around the bush.

"Our marching orders, you mean?"

Lena snorted. "Yeah."

"We don't have to go, you know," Nikki replied, her tone matter of fact. "She's not the boss of us."

"Totally not," Lena agreed.

"She tries to act like we're still kids and she's our mother, for crying out loud. We're adults. Smart, strong, *grown* women."

"Amen to that."

There was a long pause.

"So I'll see you there?"

Lena let out a long sigh.

"Yep. See you there."

9

NIKKI

Nikki opened the door to The Milky Thistle, ignoring the CLOSED sign.

She led Anna up the steps to find the bar deserted, much as she'd expected. Anna looked around, taking in the eclectic furniture and muraled ceiling with a low whistle.

"Nice place."

"Are you sure you're okay?" Nikki asked her.

Anna shot her an exasperated smile, affection and irritation all rolled up together.

"Because it's not too late," Nikki continued. "We can just go."

"I'm ready," Anna told her. She looked up at the stars, dots of paint on the high ceiling. "This is amazing. These are the actual constellations, all plotted out. Someone worked hard on this."

"That was Maddy, Gayle's daughter. Our niece."

Anna paused for a long moment.

"Another niece. Maybe I'll meet her someday." She looked back at Nikki, who looked dubious and sad all at once.

"Stop it. I'm good. I feel no kind of way about the twins. They're strangers to me. If they want to *stay* strangers to me, it's no skin off my back. I have two big sisters already, and now I have you. I'm willing to open the door to the rest of your family. If they decide to step through it, great. If not, that's their loss. I'm really good with whatever happens now that I've gotten to meet Eric."

Nikki nodded uncertainly. They'd had this conversation already once today, but she felt like she'd done an inadequate job of explaining the Axis of Evil. Anna seemed to expect a lukewarm reception at best, or a couple of cold shoulders at worst. She didn't know how bruising Jack's comments could be when he was angry. But what could Nikki do? Demand that Anna hide in her shabby living room for her entire stay? She admired her sister's bravery.

Or bravado.

Either way, she wished she could bottle it and take a sip, because all she wanted to do was turn tail and run right now.

"You're right," Nikki said reluctantly. "It would be silly to tiptoe around town and try to avoid them. We might as well all meet and just let them know that you and Dad want to get to know each other. Hopefully Lena too. If Gayle and Jack choose not to, that's their prerogative."

"Atta girl," Anna said.

A cool gust of wind came up the stairwell, and Lena came tumbling in. Her eyes widened as she spotted Anna, and she began to soft shoe backwards, waving both hands theatrically as she tried to make her exit.

"Nope." Nikki grabbed Lena's arm. "No way."

"Come on, Nik. I didn't sign up for this," Lena groaned.

"I'd braced myself for a private scolding, not full-blown fireworks."

"Who doesn't like fireworks?" asked Anna with a grin.

"Me. They stress me out. Give me some doggie tranquilizers and lock me in my kennel for the night," Lena muttered, seeming resigned. Nikki kept a firm grip on her arm, just in case.

Jo appeared from the kitchen with a platter of food. She wore her usual lumberjack combo of jeans and a threadbare plaid shirt, but somehow still looked completely at home in the classy bar. No one stood quite as tall as Jo—literally or figuratively.

"One foot out the door, Merrills?" she boomed cheerfully. "Come on inside."

Nikki took a cautious step in the direction of the large table Jo headed toward, but Lena stood rooted to the floor.

"Gayle is in the back finishing up inventory. It will take her another couple minutes, at least. She asked me to bring out the charcuterie board she prepared." Jo said this last bit with gentle irony, but the board looked amazing. Cured meats, several kinds of cheese, and the candied walnuts that Gayle made herself.

Lena perked up a little and allowed Nikki to drag her across the room.

"You must be Anna," Jo said in a neutral voice as she set the platter on the table and gestured for them to sit. "Taking the bull by the horns, huh?"

"Most of the time, yeah. I figure it beats the other end," Anna said, and Jo grinned.

"You'd fit in nicely, I'll say that much. Can I get you anything to drink?"

"Is it too early for a whiskey on the rocks?"

Nikki gave her sister a sideways glance. Anna must be more nervous than she let on. Maybe more nervous than she would admit to herself.

"Not in my book." Jo made her way to the bar and poured a glass of whiskey over ice as Nikki, Anna, and Lena each took a seat at the table.

The food in front of them looked delicious, but Nikki didn't have much of an appetite. She picked listlessly at the pomegranate slices, eating one seed at a time.

Jo came over and gave Anna her drink, and then set down two bloody marys — one for Nikki, and one for Lena.

Nikki looked up at her in surprise.

"I have a feeling you might need it," Jo said with a gentle smile.

"Thanks." Nikki took a bracing sip of the spicy drink.

"I know your sister can seem like a hardass sometimes," Jo murmured, "but try to go easy on her. Gayle just wants to protect your mom. She doesn't realize yet that she doesn't need protecting anymore."

Jo was a tough cookie — but right at the moment, her brown eyes were soft.

"She blusters like she does because she cares. Go easy," Jo said again. "And good luck to you all. I'll be pulling for you." She bustled off and disappeared into the kitchen a moment later.

"Is this stuff safe to eat, or...?" Anna trailed off with a quizzical glance.

Lena let out a little snort-laugh and nodded as Nikki took another long gulp of her drink.

"We're adults," Nikki said, as much to Lena as herself.

Lena looked at her with wide eyes. Her mouth was full of cheese and crackers as she nodded. "Yup."

"I don't give a crap what they think. I'm not running Anna out of town to appease them," Nikki added with a sniff.

Lena nodded.

"Is it cyanide that smells like almonds?" Anna mused as she studied the walnut in her hand. "Are the nuts just on there to mask the scent?"

Lena snorted with laughter, bringing a hand up to stop herself from spraying the table with cheese. Anna smiled into her whiskey.

And then Gayle walked out.

"Sorry to keep you waiting," she muttered as she strode toward the table, spearing a hand through her dark hair. "They messed up our linen order, and—"

She caught sight of Anna and stopped dead in her tracks, the color draining from her cheeks.

"Nope. No way. Nikki, are you kidding me right now?" she demanded, leveling her with a glare that could've stripped the paint off the walls.

Nikki opened her mouth to answer, but just then the door opened, bringing in a rush of brisk air.

"I don't have a lot of time. I have a class to teach at two, so let's get this over with," Jack muttered as he stepped into view. His dark brows were carved into a frown that only grew deeper as he looked around the table.

"What the hell is she doing here?" Jack demanded. "This is a family meeting—"

"And Anna is family," Nikki managed through numb lips. "Whether you two like it or not, Jack. So let's all take a seat and talk about this, shall we?"

The room went dead silent as Jack moved to turn around.

"You're just going to leave now?" she demanded, shocked she could even hear herself talk over the pounding of her heart. "Newsflash for both of you," she said, turning to flick a glance toward Gayle. "The world doesn't revolve around you. And for a family meeting, I notice someone has been omitted from the guest list. Where's Dad?" she asked with a pointed glare.

Gayle stalked closer, fastidiously avoiding glancing Anna's way, her sole focus on Nikki.

"He wasn't invited," she replied, arms crossed around her middle. "We already know how he feels, and nothing we say is going to change his mind."

"So you figured you'd bash away at poor, feeble-minded me, instead," Nikki reasoned with an incredulous laugh.

"No," Gayle shot back. "I figured I'd try to reason with you, and appeal to your good sense and better judgment." Her eyes flashed with something like pain, and Nikki flinched. "This is where we grew up, Nik. Mom and Dad's friends all live here. Do you honestly think she would want...this?" She jerked her chin in Anna's vague direction but still didn't look. "I can't believe even you would be so naive."

Nikki swallowed hard as the poison-tipped arrow struck home.

"That's uncalled for," Anna chimed in as she straightened in her seat. "I'm not trying to stick my nose where it doesn't belong, but surely all the little jabs and cruel comments aren't necc—"

"No one asked you," Jack snapped, ceasing his pacing back and forth like a caged lion to stare at Anna. "My father and sister might want you here, but the rest of us couldn't care less about your opinions. And as for you," he continued, turning back toward Nikki. "Letting her stay with you without even asking us? Bringing her to spend time with Dad in the house he shared with Mom? Unacceptable."

"I'm sorry this is so hard for you," Nikki told her brother.

His eyes were like chips of onyx, glittering and stony. He stared at her and then looked away with a snort of disgust.

"Really, Jack. I am. I didn't want to hurt you with any of this." Lord knew he'd suffered enough in his life. "But I couldn't deny myself the chance to meet our sister. And once I had, I couldn't deny Dad that chance. She looks just like him. She looks like *me*. She's family, Jack. She saved my life," Nikki added. For a second, his face seemed to soften—but it was so fleeting, she wondered if she'd imagined it. "Dad made mistakes, and Mom forgave him for those mistakes. It's time we all did too. I have the right to spend time with Anna, and so does he. You're not going to change my mind."

"No one's telling you what to do," Gayle interjected. "You made your own choice, and that's fine. But now that you have, don't expect us to support it. Or you."

Jack nodded in agreement. "She's just a walking bulletin board announcing that Dad cheated on our mother. He *betrayed* her, and then lied to all of us for years. If you can forgive that, good for you. But I'm out."

Jack turned on his heel and made swift tracks to the door.

Gayle watched him go and then turned toward Nikki.

"Happy now?" she demanded, walking away without waiting for a reply.

Happy?

No. Certainly not. In fact, she felt like she was about to

puke. But damn it, she didn't regret a thing. She had stood her ground with Jack and Gayle and was still alive to tell the tale. They were mad—furious, really—but the sky hadn't fallen down.

Somewhere, buried beneath the nausea and sadness, she felt a tiny ember of satisfaction. The deed was done. She'd told them her intentions. No more secrets. No more hiding. No more lies. They would come around, or they wouldn't. Either way, Nikki was going to live her life on her terms.

Starting today.

She put a hand on Anna's knee and managed a smile for a still-silent, semi shell-shocked-looking Lena.

"Well, that went quicker than I thought. Who wants to go shopping?"

10

ANNA

"THIS NEW RESTAURANT sounds like an absolute dream," Nikki said as she steered carefully around a bend in the road. "Just a little place overlooking the river. Farm to table. I would be able to create a new menu every week and teach the line cooks how to make everything, which means I wouldn't have to work most weekends unless I chose to."

"Which means weekends in Bluebird Bay with Mateo," Anna added, and Nikki blushed.

"And you," she said. "But yeah, it makes the long-distance thing with Mateo a lot more realistic. Or less, when I think about how hard it would be to leave this job if we ever decided to move in together."

"That man would walk through fire for you," Anna told her sister. "He basically did already. You two are going to be fine. I can feel it in my bones."

"Thanks." Nikki seemed to relax a bit. They were silent for a moment, enjoying the scenery on the narrow country road. Deciduous trees stood stark and statuesque against an evergreen backdrop, and the sky was a pale blue. A tremor ran through her as she thought of the day ahead, but she pushed it aside. There was nothing to be nervous about. She and Eric had broken the ice the other night at dinner and had seen each other twice since then, albeit never just the two of them. This would be a first.

It had been an interesting few days. After the explosive meeting with all of her Cherry Blossom Point siblings, the twins had basically fallen off the radar. No more texts from Jack to Nikki, and, according to Lena, Gayle had stopped blowing up her phone. It had been crickets. She wasn't sure if it was a permanent decision or if they were in the eye of a hurricane. Whatever the case, Jack and Gayle seemed determined to pretend that Anna had never been born. That was fine by her. As much as she didn't appreciate the tone they'd taken with Nikki, she actually had some real sympathy for them both. She understood where they were coming from, and had felt much the same way when Nikki had come to find her in Bluebird Bay.

She shot a glance at her sister. Despite Nikki's brave face, Anna could tell that her oldest siblings' stony silence was weighing on her.

At least Lena had come around. She had finally decided to get off the fence, choosing to side with Nikki and Anna, and it had been the three of them ever since. Things had been tense between them right after the family meeting, but within an hour Lena had loosened up. Anna had talked her into trying on a sexy cocktail dress for an upcoming function, and Lena had turned nearly as red as the fabric when Anna greeted her with a wolf whistle. This new sister of hers was a bombshell, and she was a *character.* Perfectly imperfect and not afraid to laugh — at the world or at herself. Plus, she had endless stories about her boss that made Anna laugh until her sides ached – and excellent taste in movies, to boot. The three of them had stayed up late the night before, marathoning old musicals and black-and-white films at Nikki's place.

Anna had even gotten to meet Lena's Irish hunk, Owen.

Did no one else see how the man looked at her? Seemed not. Maybe it was Anna's outsider's perspective; everyone else had known Owen since his prepubescent days. But good lord, the man was a dish. More importantly, he was obviously crazy about Lena. There was a tension there, but also the deep easiness that came from knowing a person for decades.

Maybe Lena needed a nudge...not that Anna would be doing the nudging. She was already at the center of enough drama. Besides, Lena probably had her reasons for keeping the gorgeous Irishman at arm's length.

"This is the place." Nikki's voice pulled Anna from her reverie as they turned into a small parking lot. "And there's Dad's car."

"I can't wait to hear about your interview," Anna told her. "They're going to love you. Break a leg."

"You too," Nikki said reflexively, and then covered her mouth with a gasp. "Wait, that's a terrible thing to say to someone before they go on a hike. Good luck, I meant. Not that you need it."

"Thanks," Anna said with a grin, wondering which of them was more nervous about the day ahead. "I'll see you at home for lunch," she added and climbed out of the car just as Eric pulled up in his hatchback.

"See you then!"

Nikki gave a friendly honk and a wave to her dad before driving off.

Eric popped the car into park and stepped out a moment later, a wide smile on his face.

He made his way toward her but stopped a few feet away, seeming to vacillate between embracing Anna and giving her space.

"I'm so glad you came."

"I'm always down for a walk in the woods," she replied, hoping she didn't sound as nervous as she felt.

"Me too." Eric smiled. "No camera today?"

She shook her head ruefully. "I've been told I get a little lost behind the lens sometimes. I wanted to make sure I was...present today."

Eric was giving her that adoring new-father look again, and Anna's cheeks grew warm. She turned towards the woods.

"Which way to the trailhead?"

"Over here." Eric led the way to a narrow dirt path through the forest.

It was a gorgeous morning, sunny and brisk but not freezing. Anna took in her surroundings with an open attention that she rarely practiced. So often, she got sidetracked by a bit of Spanish moss draped over a tree limb or the way the light filtered through a leaf that had been chewed up by a caterpillar, creating a stained-glass window made by Mother Nature herself. She would take photo after photo, captured by that tiny moment. It was amazing, and it was one of her greatest passions. But how many times had she missed the forest for the trees?

"That's a dark-eyed junco," Eric told her, pointing at a

sweet little gray bird. "Some people think they're drab, but they've always been one of my favorites." The sparrow flitted away with a flash of white tail feathers.

"She was adorable," Anna agreed, smiling as they walked on. "Sometimes the less flashy animals are my favorite to photograph. There's something magical about the ones that seem so in tune and can blend in with their surroundings. They seem completely at home and content being exactly where they are. Being a bit of a wanderer and someone who struggled with that for a long time, they give me a sense of peace."

She cleared her throat, a little embarrassed of how open she'd been, but Eric slowed to a stop and nodded solemnly.

"I know what you mean. I always loved to travel. Didn't get to do it much, what with a big family and finances being tight back then, but loved it nonetheless. Then, as I grew older and the kids grew up, I realized there is something really grounding about having a hometown, a place to come to where people know your name."

His brow furrowed and he shoved a hand in his pocket.

"I wanted—" Eric paused and shook his head. "I just want to apologize for what happened the other day. Lena told me what happened, and I'm sorry Gayle wasn't more welcoming. She can be prickly. Jack too. He's like a wounded bear who just can't seem to figure out how to heal, and he swipes those giant paws at those around him sometimes."

She tucked that nugget away to chew on later as she nodded. "I get it," Anna said. Eric gave her a worried glance and she said, "Really, I do. I was just thinking about it on my way here. I didn't exactly welcome Nikki into my life with open arms, when she came to town. She's forgiven me for it, but I still feel like a heel when I think about it."

"I'm sure it was a shock. I'm sorry you had to go through that."

"It's fine," Anna said with a shrug. "And, in the end, it was worth it. Maybe they'll come around, and maybe they won't. But I have two little sisters, and meeting you... it's enough."

"It's not fine," Eric said with a force that startled her. He continued in a softer voice, sorrow-filled eyes on the skyline. "What I did...it wasn't *fine*. Anna, I look at you and my heart breaks, thinking of all of the years I missed. And then it breaks again with the sheer joy of having you here in front of me. I hardly know what to say to you. I only know that I'll never be able to make it up to you. Even so, I'm going to try."

She turned away, emotion welling up in her throat, and began to walk slowly. Eric fell into step at her side.

"I've thought about it a lot," she said when she could finally speak. "And I don't think you have anything to be sorry for, on that front. I had a wonderful childhood. Two sisters who mothered me half to death and a dad who treated me exactly the same as his biological children. I wouldn't change a thing about my life," she said with a shrug. "Truly. I had so many amazing adventures, and I finally found love... even a grandson, which I never thought I'd be lucky enough to have. I was too busy traveling to have kids. Nieces and nephews were enough for me. But getting to do the baby thing with Teddy without actually being tied to a kid twenty-four/seven...What I'm trying to say is that my life turned out pretty perfect. I can't blame you and my mom for choosing your marriages and your older children — not to mention your spouses and your homes and your *peace* — over telling the absolute truth."

Well... she could, Anna reflected silently. But she wouldn't. Cancer had taken her mother and then a piece of Anna herself. She had lost two parents already, and she had come close to death more than once. Time was precious and promised to no one, and she knew one thing for sure. She wasn't going to waste any more of it on anger and resentment.

"I'm grateful for the childhood that I had, *and* I'm grateful that Nikki insisted on meeting me. I'm glad to know you, Eric."

"I'm glad to know you too, Anna," Eric replied. "More than I can say."

When Anna glanced over at her biological father, she saw that his eyes were full of tears an instant before he turned away and pointed up into a tree.

"You hear that?" he asked, pausing. "There's a tufted titmouse up there somewhere."

Anna laughed at the funny name, brushing away the tears that had gathered in her own eyes. She stood next to Eric and looked up into the branches of the tree.

"They are amazing creatures," Eric whispered. "They're so small, but they're very hardy for their size. They can withstand the brutal winters because they hide food in tree crevices and behind loose pieces of bark to come back and find later, when pickings are slim."

A small movement drew her gaze to a tiny plump gray bird with a blush patch under its wing. The titmouse had a dramatic silver triangle on the top of its head, like a little shark fin. Its face and belly were white, with a black stripe above its beak. The bird bounced back and forth along the branch, head tilting this way and that as it peered down at them. It was even more adorable than the sparrow they had seen.

Her fingers twitched, aching for her camera. She realized with a start that it was the first time that had happened since they started their outing.

She'd been present.

Nice.

They walked on for another hour or so, chatting easily about birds, nature, and Anna's travels. As the sun rose higher in the sky, Eric's pace began to slow.

Anna stopped and put a gentle hand on his shoulder. "Are you feeling alright?"

"My arthritis is acting up some," Eric admitted. "It does that, in the wintertime. The cold gets in your bones at my age."

"Let's start back," Anna said quickly, making a mental note. Eric was mentally very quick and astute, but he was deep into his seventh decade. She didn't want him to push too hard.

They took a shorter, straighter path back to the parking lot and arrived half an hour later. He unlocked the car and they both climbed in, red-cheeked and smiling.

"That was a lot of fun," Eric said as he plugged the keys into the ignition. "I'm usually alone when I go birding, so it was a real treat for me. I guess I'll drop you back at Nikki's place now?"

Something about his tone made Anna shake her head.

"Actually, do you want to stop and warm up with a hot cup of tea or coffee?" Anna asked impulsively.

"I'd love to." Eric grinned as he pulled out of the lot and onto the road. "Do you like hot chocolate?"

"Do titmouses have mohawks? Of course I do!" she shot back with a wink. "Wait...would it be titmouses or titmice?" she asked, shooting him an arched brow.

He laughed out loud and cranked up the heat. "I'll have to get back to you on that one."

Eric drove them to Nunnery Street, which basically constituted most of Cherry Blossom Point's downtown area. Anna looked the other way as they passed The Milky Thistle. Luckily, he didn't stop driving until they were another half mile down the road. Eric scored a curbside spot further on, and led her into a sweet little cafe.

"This place has been here for years," he told her as they walked in. "They serve frozen hot chocolate — I never really understood that term, but let me tell you, it's delicious — in the summertime, and hot chocolate the rest of the year."

"Mayan hot chocolate," Anna read from the board. "Single-source cacao and cayenne. Yum. I know what I'm getting."

They approached the counter, where an older woman with blue-black hair beamed at them through a pair of coke-bottle glasses.

"Eric!" she said cheerfully. "Great to see you. And Nikki! I haven't seen you in—" She stopped mid-sentence and stared at Anna in confusion. "Oh. I'm sorry. I thought you were... someone else."

What was it Eric had been saying about a hometown where people knew your name?

Silence hung between the three of them and Anna quickly filled it. "Hi, I'm Anna. It's nice to meet you."

Eric looked stricken for a brief moment and Anna half-wondered if he would turn and walk out the door. Then he smiled.

"Frannie, Anna is my daughter. I've been so blessed to finally connect with her. She's visiting from Bluebird Bay."

The woman stared in silence for a long moment, and then returned his smile with a slow nod.

"Well, I can certainly see the resemblance. What can I get you two?"

"One of your Mayan hot chocolates, please, and one of the mint," Eric said, ordering for them both. "Also, two of each of today's chocolate creams." Frannie handed him the latter and he led Anna to a table, bearing a plate with six misshapen lumps that looked not unlike the chocolate droppings sold in joke shops.

"They taste a lot better than they look," Eric said as they sat down.

He ate the dark chocolate cream in one huge bite. The white chocolate looked less intimidating, and Anna bit the top off one of those. There was a thin shell of chocolate around an interior of luscious, rose-flavored whipped cream.

"So good," she murmured, and took another bite.

Frannie delivered their drinks, and as Anna looked up to thank her, she realized that two patrons were watching her from a nearby table, whispering. They looked quickly away when she met their eyes, and the chatter ceased, but there was no question they'd been talking about her.

She took a sip of her hot drink, but hardly tasted it.

"Are you all right?" she asked a now pensive-looking Eric quietly.

He reached over and patted her hand. "Don't you worry

about me. I'm fine. I'm just worried about *you*. Are you all right?"

She nodded, but she couldn't give voice to the white lie.

She wasn't all right. In fact, she was a little shaken up. For some reason, she hadn't really thought (or cared) about the reactions of other people in the town, despite the twins' protests. Now, in the harsh light of day, she couldn't help but wonder if coming out in public with her father had been a mistake. Maybe it would be better if they stuck to the woods in the future.

They finished their chocolate creams, but in the end Anna transferred the lion's share of their hot chocolates into to-go cups. And as they walked back to the car, she couldn't stop the seeds of doubt from sprouting in her heart.

Maybe the twins were right.

Maybe it wasn't fair to act like her existence hadn't nearly destroyed a family. *Their* family. Whether it was her intention or not, the facts remained. She was a stranger, coming into their safe haven, their peace, their home, and kicking up all sorts of mud.

Current relationship status with father number two?

Complicated.

11

LENA

"THIS IS A DISASTER!" Freddie exclaimed for the fourth time in the past hour. "These matchsticks are a completely different size."

"It's the same brand," Lena repeated patiently. "Same box."

Frederick held up two identical matches, just inches from Lena's face. She raised one brow, and he took a step back. Still, he held the matches at her eye level. His expression was an almost comical mix of persecution and despair.

"How can I work under these conditions? Neither the width nor the thickness are the same. It will completely undermine the structural integrity of the project."

"I can contact the manufacturer first thing Monday morning and see what they say."

Lena glanced at her watch. She still had to run home to change before heading over to Owen's show, which meant that she needed to leave ASAP. Freddie knew that full well, which made this meltdown utterly predictable.

"I can't start over with a different brand," he whined. "I'll have wasted nearly sixty hours of work."

And that's only counting your *hours,* Lena thought grimly.

"I'll never have time to complete the project by opening night if I have to start from scratch."

"You could always paint something."

Lena's gaze drifted up the stairs to the one spot of glorious color in the room.

Fluidity.

She could never understand why he didn't stick to the one thing he did so brilliantly.

"I cannot just *paint* something!" Freddie exclaimed. "I want to create something new! Something three-dimensional. Something unique. Painting is so passé," he groaned, slumping onto his stiff, uncomfortable gray sofa.

Freddie's private rooms upstairs were plush and comfy. Lena had commissioned the pieces herself, furniture custom-made to his liking. But the main room, the place where Lena spent her days, was something between an art museum and a prison. Which was exactly what he needed to keep him on task.

"I suggest that you put a pin in this and just try to enjoy your weekend," Lena said with a sigh. "Like I said, I'll contact the company first thing next week and get the lot numbers figured out. Maybe this other batch is from a different factory. I'm sure we can get our hands on some matchsticks that are exactly the same as the ones you've been using. Leave it to me."

Lena's phone buzzed and she pulled it out of the pocket of her jeans.

Sunday Funday??? It was a text from Anna. *Me and Nikki are going to brunch tomorrow at eleven. You in?*

Definitely, Lena texted back.

She had been so scared of what would happen if Anna came to town — and the twins' reaction had been pretty much exactly what she'd expected — but her new sister was impossible not to like. She had a great sense of humor and an endless treasure trove of adventure stories. Polar bears and rainforest hikes and trips down the Nile. Sure, she was a tiny bit bossy — Lena flushed as she thought of the uncharacteristically sexy dress her sisters had convinced her to buy for tonight — but in a fun, encouraging way. Anna acted the way she'd always dreamed an older sister would.

Her thoughts drifted to Gayle. She could be such a steamroller. But Lena couldn't deny it.

She missed her.

With a swipe of her thumb, she switched over to her text thread with Gayle to see if she'd missed a recent message, but there was nothing. Radio silence since the mandatory family meeting text earlier in the week.

It was so weird not hearing from her every day, or seeing her for a meal and a catch up chat...

Jack had gone AWOL as well. Lena drove past his house every night on her way home from work, and his truck hadn't been in the driveway. The lights in his house had been off for days, ever since the family meeting that he'd declared to be nothing of the sort. She didn't understand how he could look into Anna's face — a face that was so eerily similar to both Nikki and Dad — and still treat her this way. But that was Jack. She shouldn't be surprised. He was probably having a good stew in a cave somewhere.

"I'm not paying you to sext with Ireland's answer to Chris Evans, you know," Freddie said suddenly.

"*Excuse* me?" Lena stared at him in disbelief.

"That's him, right? Telling you to get off of work early and come to his show?"

"Early?" she exclaimed. "It's nearly seven PM on a Saturday!"

"We have an artistic emergency! I can't wait til midway through the week for a company that doesn't even bother to ensure that their products are of equal size. I need you to go to the store and compare this matchstick to—"

"Absolutely not, Freddie. *You* go if it's so important to you."

"*Me?* In a hardware store?"

By his horrified expression, one would think she'd suggested he go to crocodile river and swim naked.

He let out a snort of disgust. "Really, Lena."

She held up one hand and took a calming breath as she turned away.

"I'm done for the day. I'm leaving. I'll see you on Monday."

"What? No way!"

He sounded like a child having a tantrum. Normally, she'd let him have his way just so she didn't have to hear it, but her patience was at an end.

She wheeled back toward him and looked him dead in the eye. "Enough! Get it together this instant or you can find another Girl Friday to be at your beck and call seventy hours a week. Understood?"

Freddie dropped to his knees and clasped his hands

together with typical high drama. "You would leave me like that? Lena, say it isn't so!"

"Frederick, geez, get up—" Lena began, exasperated.

"Okay. Okay, I'm sorry," he interrupted her. "I'm really truly madly terribly sorry. I would be lost without you, and you know it. Forgive me."

"Forgiven," she said shortly. "Now pull yourself together and step away from this for a while," she said, gesturing to the mess in front of her. "We can revisit it Monday. Have a nice rest of your weekend, *Freddie*."

With that, she grabbed her coat and purse, turned, and walked out.

It wasn't the first time she'd put her foot down with him, but she had to admit, it was the *best* time. One of the better by-products of the blowout with the twins had been this strange new sense of freedom. Like she was beginning to emerge from some self-created cocoon that would allow her to say what she needed to say without living in terror that the world was going to collapse around her. She wondered idly if Nikki was feeling the same way and resolved to ask her.

But first, she had a party to get to.

She glanced at her watch as she jogged to the car. If she met him at the gallery, she just might make it close to on time.

Freddie kept me late, she texted before starting her car. *Meet you there.*

She drove home — past her brother's still-empty house — and stripped off her clothes. A brush made her hair look entirely too big and entirely too eighties, but a second go at it after she smoothed it with a bit of oil tamed her curls somewhat. She shrugged and headed for her closet. In record time, she'd donned the dress that Anna had convinced her to buy. It was just as well that she had no time to primp and preen for too long. Even five more minutes would've had her second-guessing the fitted dress in a head-turning shade of crimson.

After a quick swipe of clear gloss and a dab of mascara and blush, she was out the door.

Despite her quick-change routine, Lena was twenty minutes late by the time she got to the gallery. She rushed through the door, breathless, and saw Owen standing near the back, completely surrounded by a throng of people. He was wearing a black cable-knit sweater and a fitted pair of chinos, which was about as dressed up as Owen got. And she had to admit, he looked gorgeous. More like a renegade fisherman, fit from hauling in massive nets, than an artist at his own exhibition.

More people scuttled toward him, nearly eclipsing him from view, and she nodded to herself.

Okay, so she might be late, but the rest of the crowd had clearly been much more punctual. The place was packed.

Lena grinned as she scanned all the faces, some familiar, most not. A thrill of excitement went through her. Maybe this would finally be Owen's big break.

She said hello to a few acquaintances and snatched a flute of golden bubbly from a passing waiter on her way over to the artist himself, but then she stopped short. She would literally have to elbow her way through the crowd—mostly female, she noted with an eyeroll—fawning over him and his work.

Lena recognized one of the women, a statuesque redhead wearing an emerald green dress she looked like she'd been poured into. A journalist named Victoria Lavorando. She wrote for the Maine Sunday Telegram. The woman had penned a scathing review of Freddie's rubber ducky exhibit that had put him in a funk for nearly a month. She'd called it *"uninspired at best, ludicrous at worst"* and written that the only thing Frederick had gotten right was the title. *"The arteest rubba-dub-dubbed this exhibit 'Rubber Duckies, Only Sadder', and boy, was he spot on. The makers of the iconic bath toy that brought joy to millions would be weeping if they could see this mess of an installation."*

While she wasn't wrong, Lena still held it against her. As much as she wanted to throttle Freddie at times, he was still like family to her.

Really screwed up, dysfunctional family.

Soooo, exactly like real family, she thought with a wry smile.

She was about to turn away and check out the exhibit until Owen was able to free himself, but then paused. Was Victoria kissing Owen's ear right now?

Lena's fingers tightened reflexively over the delicate flute, and she had to will herself to relax her grip for fear of it shattering.

Just then, the redhead tossed her head back and let out a throaty laugh at something Owen said. Worse? He grinned back at her as she closed one manicured hand over his bare forearm.

For a journalist, she sure seemed much more interested in Owen than his artwork...

Stop being a shrew. He's not yours, she reminded herself firmly.

Lena turned away and grabbed a shrimp puff off the tray of hors d'oeuvres.

She wandered around, checking out the displays... but as much as she adored Owen's art, she suddenly wished she was anywhere else. Her feet ached after running around for Freddie all day, and she felt ridiculous in this bright red dress, wandering around solo. She never should have let her sisters talk her into something so flashy. Not that it mattered. Owen hadn't even noticed her in the crowd.

"Hello again," a low voice murmured from behind her. "Fancy seeing you here."

She turned to find Guillermo standing there with a welcoming smile.

"Hello there. Small world!" Lena said, trying for a polite voice rather than the grim resignation that she felt.

"I'm not familiar with the artist, but a colleague told me I might be able to get some serious holiday shopping done for the special lady in my life," he leaned closer and winked, "my mom." She smiled politely and nodded before he continued in a rush. "I don't suppose you'd consent to give me a tour?"

Why had she let Owen sway her into spending her few Freddie-free hours around more artists? She shot a glance toward her friend and found him exactly where she'd left him: in Victoria's clutches and looking none the worse for wear about it. He didn't need her here; that was obvious. She would rather be at home on her couch watching *My Fair Lady* and wearing nothing but her bathrobe.

It was only the realization that she sounded like Eeyore from Winnie the Pooh that had a grin tugging at her lips. She got exactly one and a half days off per week. She wasn't about to squander any more of it moping around.

"Sure," she replied.

It wasn't like she had anything better to do...

She led him to the corner where the different ornaments were displayed and showed him her favorites. "It's so fragile, but just look how intense the color is," she said, eyes riveted to one in particular. It was an arresting interplay of green reflections and white light that dripped down in the shape of a flame rather than the more traditional, round ornament.

"Enchanting," Guillermo murmured, his gaze glued to her instead of the ornament.

Drat this dress.

Lena felt color rise to her cheeks. This was definitely not the attention she was hoping to get...

She moved away from Guillermo under the guise of showing him the plates Owen had made, but a woman's voice had her slowing her step.

"Lena!"

"Hey, Sheree!" Lena faced the gallery owner, hoping the relief didn't show on her face.

"You look absolutely stunning."

"This exhibit is stunning," Lena deflected.

"Hey, if you have time, maybe early next week, I could use your eye. I have some new paintings coming in from a watercolor artist named Ellie Welsh. I think she might be special."

"Oh my gosh! I love her," Lena gasped.

"You know her?" Sheree cocked her head, dark brows knitted.

"I saw a couple of her paintings at a festival last year. I was tempted to snatch them all up—she was asking a pittance, far less than they were worth—but I just didn't have the wall space. I've regretted it ever since. They were some of the most extraordinary watercolors I've ever seen. Is she in town?" Lena asked eagerly.

"No, I couldn't convince her to come. She's something of a recluse," Sheree said with a shake of her head. "But she's interested in showing her stuff here."

"Snatch her up, for sure," Lena replied. "She's going places."

Someone bumped into her, jostling her champagne glass, and moved away with a muttered apology.

"You've gathered quite the crowd tonight!"

Sheree beamed with satisfaction. "It's quite a show."

"It really is."

She realized with a start that Guillermo was still standing beside her. "I'm so sorry, Sheree, this is Guillermo. Guillermo, this is Sheree, the owner of the gallery."

He stepped around Lena and held out his hand to Sheree.

"I dabble some, myself, in oils," he told her. "I would love to show you some of my—"

"Oh, Johnny handles acquisitions," Sheree said. "I just enjoy the art."

"You know," Lena mused, "now that I think about Ellie's paintings, I think they could have a super wide appeal as far as decor and such." She was talking mostly to herself, but Sheree looked at her with interest as she pressed on. "Prints, for sure, but what about greeting cards? People love to buy beautiful paintings, but unique and truly stunning cards are more manageable, for most. Eight by ten, so it can be framed. Like a card and a gift in one."

Sheree blinked and nodded. "Geez, that's a good idea. I'll see if Johnny can put you in contact with the artist. If you can talk her into it, I'd be more than willing to front the cost of the printing. Something like that would be a wonderful idea for a recluse who can't promote herself or come to her own opening."

"I understand the impulse," said a voice with a familiar brogue.

Lena turned to find Owen staring at her, looking sexy and slightly disheveled. Well. No doubt an hour with Victoria had that effect on a man.

Sheree let out a chuckle. "You're doing just fine, Owen." An interested buyer flagged her down and she turned and gave them a quick finger wiggle. "Duty calls," she said before slipping away into the crowd.

Owen stepped forward and gave her a quick peck on the cheek.

"Hey, love. So glad you came. I'm sorry it took me so long to escape the mob." Then he looked at Guillermo, and his eyes went flat. "I don't believe we've met."

"Owen, this is Guillermo," Lena said. "He's a friend of Frederick's."

"Well then," Owen said in a strange, low voice. "Any friend of Freddie's is a...friend of Freddie's."

Lena frowned at him and turned back to Guillermo. "This is Owen McKenna."

"Ah, so all this is yours, then? The Christmas baubles and plates and all?"

Apparently, Guillermo felt Owen's derision and had decided to bite back a little.

Good for him.

The corner of Owen's mouth kicked up and he nodded. "Yup. That's me. The bauble maker."

Lena smiled at Guillermo and said, "It was lovely to see you again. If you'll excuse us? I just need to introduce Owen to a friend."

"Of course," he replied. "I didn't mean to monopolize your time."

Lena took Owen's arm in a pincer grip and steered him away from the crowd, then looked up at him with a raised eyebrow and exaggerated head tilt.

"Sorry," he said immediately.

"What is going on with you? I'm sorry I was late, but that's no reason to be rude to my friend."

"I know, I'm sorry," Owen said again, raking his hand over his face with a sigh. "I'm just on edge with this much publicity. Can we get some air?"

"Sure." They wound their way through the crowd until they were outside. The clear December air was like ambrosia after the stuffy heat of the crowded gallery.

"First off, you look gorgeous," Owen said. His tone was unusually serious, and Lena looked at him in surprise. "I'm not kidding, love. That dress is something else on you."

"It's something else, all right. And I can't wait to get it off."

His ocean blue eyes went stormy and her whole body went hot, despite her coat still being in the car.

She willed herself to say something, anything, to break the tension that was so hypnotic, it had her wanting to lean closer and—

"I've got to go," she blurted in a rush. "I, um, I had a really long day with Freddie. Plus, my feet are killing me in these shoes, and I think I've had as much socializing as I can handle for the night. Would you mind if I just head home?"

A fleeting look of disappointment danced across his beautiful face, but then he smiled. "Of course not. I'm just glad you came at all. Let me walk you to your car."

She wanted nothing more than to sprint away...from him *and* her confounding feelings, but there was no way to decline gracefully that wouldn't seem weird. Still, she was pretty sure her already terrible poker face was on its last legs, and the sooner she got out of arm's reach of this man, the better.

When they reached her car, he opened the door for her and stepped back.

"I'm so proud of you, Owen," she said truthfully. "Your exhibit is phenomenal. It's a bona fide hit. Now let's see if Victoria writes about it."

Just the name left a bitter taste on her tongue, but she forced a smile.

"As long as you think it's great, that's the most important thing to me," Owen said, stepping close and pulling her in for a tight squeeze. "I swear, until I saw your face across the room, I felt like I was holding my breath. There was this knot of stress in my stomach. Truly... I know you had a long day at work and have your own family stuff going on, and I really appreciate you coming."

She breathed in his familiar, woodsy smell, and then released him reluctantly. Only, Owen didn't let go. He pulled back just enough to look into her eyes, leaving his hands resting on her hips.

Her heart careened out of control and she began to babble as she stepped away. "Okay, so, uh, it was really fun. Again, great job. You killed it!" She shot him with a pair of finger-guns and even made the "*pyew pyew*" sound to go along with them. "See you later, alligator," she added as she stumbled off the curb against the car, because why not make it even worse?

Owen grinned and shook his head with a chuckle. "Be careful you don't hurt yourself there, love."

"I'm good. Great, in fact. All set. Talk to you tomorrow," she said as she slid into the driver's seat and waved him off.

For the next thirty seconds, Lena sat in her car, trembling, as she watched him walk down the street. What the hell had that been about?

The look in his eyes when he'd held her... the way he'd put his hands on her hips—

No.

No way.

She was reading too much into it. This was Owen. Middle school projects, high school shenanigans, family-functions Owen.

Her mind was playing tricks on her...

Wasn't it?

12

GAYLE

It was nearly closing time at The Milky Thistle. Technically it was *past* closing time, but three regulars sat chatting at one of the community tables, and there was a couple in deep conversation in the back corner beneath the undulating neon lights of the aurora borealis. The kitchen was closed and the staff had gone home.

It was just Gayle and Jo left at the end of a long shift. Either one of them could close up on her own, but neither was in a hurry to get home. Jo's apartment was empty — her pit bull, Pixie, was currently asleep under the table just a couple feet away — and Gayle's house was equally uninviting. The Milky Thistle felt more like home to both women than did the places where they slept each night.

"A game this high stakes, I wonder why you don't practice more," Jo teased as Gayle collected her darts from the board... and the wall behind it.

"I practice every day. I get here an hour before you do just to work on my form," Gayle lied. "One of these days, I'm going to whoop your butt. Wait and see."

Jo snorted and threw a dart. It hit the target just left of dead center.

She was the undisputed queen of darts, and only suckers played her for money. Gayle only did it because Jo refused to accept compensation for all of the extra hours that she worked outside of her time at the bar. Between researching new drinks and stopping in on her rare days off to hop behind the bar and give Gayle a break, she deserved more than her salary. High-stakes darts was a way for Gayle to pad her friend's income without argument. Plus, it gave them an excuse to hang around past the bar's official closing time. One of their customers' favorite things about the bar was that no one ever pushed them out the door. Either Gayle or Jo was always happy to stay until the last customer was gone. Usually they both stayed. At some point, when the crowd was gone, Jo always ran home and came back with her sweet-tempered pup, who was a customer favorite. Gayle leaned down and patted Pixie's square head.

"Who's a good girl?"

Pixie grinned at her as if to say, *"It's me,"* and Gayle smiled back.

She was always so grateful to have both the dog and her owner around, even more so in times like these. She missed her family terribly. Having her siblings and Beth in Cherry Blossom Point had made the absence of her own children so much easier to bear. The past few days had been torture. Still, she knew if she spoke to Nikki or Lena, she would end up yelling at them, so she didn't call them at all. Jack had been MIA since the "family" meeting, and she couldn't even work up the stomach to call her father.

She definitely couldn't go to his house for fear of running

into what's her face... she looked like a flat-chested, slightly older Nikki. It was just too *Twilight Zone.*

"Another round?" Gayle asked as Jo collected her darts from the center of the board.

"Nah, I'm tired of wiping the floor with you." Jo smiled. "Anyway, I want to mix up those new drinks for you to try for next week's specials. Come on over to the bar."

Gayle did as she was told, and Pixie followed. The ten-year-old pit bull flopped down beside her barstool with a happy sigh. So long as she could be near her people, she was content.

Gayle so felt that right now.

"I made some new simple syrups," Jo said as she mixed a drink. "This rosemary-clove syrup could go with a lot of things, but for this week I'm thinking hot apple cider and rum. You'll have to use your imagination for the heat, because I am too damn lazy to go heat you some cider."

The cider Jo pulled from the fridge was also homemade and perfectly spiced. Together with the syrup and rum, it was comfort in a glass.

"This is absolute money," Gayle told her. "Delicious."

"This next syrup is the best I've made in a long time," said Jo without a trace of false modesty. "Blackberry lavender. Taste it in some seltzer and tell me what you think."

Gayle took a sip and was instantly transported to a balmy day on the beach. "Oh wow, Jo. It tastes like summer. So fresh and crisp."

"I know, right? But what should we make with it? Nothing I've come up with so far has been quite right."

"Something simple." Gayle stood and came around to the back of the bar. "We can add it to a gimlet? The tart lime and the sweet berry would be awesome together. Or maybe a French 75?"

"I like your thinking." Jo grabbed two bottles. "Champagne and just a touch of gin. Try that."

"Decadent," Gayle said as she sipped. "Like something they'd serve at an afternoon summer wedding."

"Too delicate for our clientele?"

"Nah, we get enough youngsters and out of towners to balance the scales. Anyway, you're not the most delicate flower in the bouquet and you love it."

"This is true," Jo acknowledged with a grin.

"Okay, my turn." Gayle dug out a bottle she had hidden behind the bar and held it up to the light. It shone a gorgeous sapphire blue.

"What is *that*?" Jo demanded, wide-eyed.

"Vodka and dried flowers, something called butterfly pea. They don't taste like much, so it's versatile. We could use some of your lighter-colored simple syrups. The fennel, maybe? Or the lemon verbena?"

"Or just keep it simple. Butterfly martinis? Blue vodka tonics? Does it turn purple if you add cranberry juice?"

"Cranberry juice gets a little muddy, but I can get a gorgeous royal purple by adding hibiscus tea. And look at this." Gayle poured some of the bright blue vodka into a glass of seltzer and then added a squeeze of lemon. The acidic juice swirled through the drink, turning it a bright pink.

"Oh, we're going to have fun with this one." Jo picked it up and took a sip. "Refreshing but also gorgeous. We could float some lychee pearls inside."

"Perfect," Gayle agreed, picking up her Blackberry-Lavender French 75. They clinked their glasses and drank.

"Oh, before I forget to tell you, I'm going to need a few days off before Christmas," Jo said. "I'm going to my sister's place in Vermont."

Gayle glanced at her in surprise. "Don't you usually spend Christmas with your cousin Ashley?"

"I usually do, yeah." Jo stared up at the painted ceiling. After a long pause, she said, "Ashley's dead, Gayle."

A wave of shock rolled through her as the words sank in. "Oh my God, no. Jo," Gayle put a hand on her friend's arm, "I'm so sorry. When did she pass away?"

Jo trailed her finger over the rim of her glass, unwilling to meet Gayle's gaze.

"Twenty-six years ago."

Gayle's mind raced as she set her drink down with a *thunk.* "But... I don't understand."

"I've never told anyone this story. Not even you. Ashley... She's the reason I moved here. There were too many memories back home. It was just too painful."

Jo circled around to the other side of the bar, pausing to pet Pixie before she took a seat on one of the stools. Gayle leaned on the bar across from her friend, prepping herself to hear something devastating.

"Ashley and I grew up together," Jo said slowly, eyes on her drink. "She was more of a sister to me than my own sister, because Marie is so much older than me and Ashley was a couple years younger. She was my shadow. The younger sister I never had. She followed me everywhere. We spent our whole childhoods together, and our houses were just two blocks apart. Her mom, my Auntie Kate, passed away when Ash was only twelve, so after that she basically lived with us because her dad was pretty useless."

Jo paused and took a sip of her drink, then continued, her tone matter of fact.

"When I was twenty-eight and she was a few weeks shy of twenty-six, we had a terrible fight, just three days before Christmas. I was so angry that I wouldn't answer her calls, didn't speak to her for days. I was hosting Christmas that year and she didn't show up, and didn't call the next day. I felt bad I'd let my anger ruin the holiday, so I went to see her with her gift in hand to make it right." Her throat worked as she swallowed hard and continued. "When I got there, her car was in the driveway, but she didn't open the door when I knocked. I had a key, so I let myself in. I found her in her bed... and she wasn't moving." Jo took a deep breath. "Ashley was a type-one diabetic. She had some infection that flew under the radar and it caused her sugar to spike so high it put her into a diabetic coma... She never woke up."

"I am so sorry, Jo," Gayle said softly, wishing she knew what else to say. There were no words that could help. She knew that from her own experience with loss.

"She was nearly twenty-six when she died. I've lived without her for as long as I knew her, now. It's such a grim, bizarre milestone... I never forgave myself for not picking up when she called. For not checking in on her on Christmas. For years — for *decades*, Gayle — I'd ask myself 'What did she want to tell me? Did she need help? Did she know she was sick? Was she afraid?'" Jo's voice wavered, and she looked away.

Heartsick, Gayle reached across the bar and took Jo's hand, but Jo pulled away and took another sip of her drink.

"Sorry, I've got to just push through to get to the end," she said with an apologetic smile. "Because what I need to explain is that I've spent the past twenty-six Christmases with Ashley. Every year, I would drive home and stay with my folks, but while they had their Christmas dinner, I would go sit at the cemetery with Ashley. I brought hot cider—she always loved hot cider— because I just couldn't let her spend Christmas alone. Not again. I even kept going after my parents passed away. Still trying to make up for the Christmas that I missed. But there's no going back, Gayle." Jo looked her friend in the eye. "Nothing I do now can ever replace *that* Christmas. So I've decided that this year, I'm going to try to release it. I'm going to let Ash rest in peace, and give myself permission to focus on the living."

"Geez, Jo," Gayle croaked, wiping her eyes. "God, I can't imagine how that must feel."

"I *want* you to imagine it," Jo said in a harsh voice.

Gayle drew back, stung. Jo's expression softened as she took Gayle's hand.

"I hope to God you never experience that kind of pain. But I want you to imagine it. Do you understand?" She shook her head and let out a harsh bark of a laugh. "I don't even remember what the fight was about. Because it doesn't even matter. It probably didn't matter *then,* either. But I let it steal something precious from me, and I don't want to see you do the same thing. Now, I'm not telling you to be a doormat or let someone walk all over you. But I *am* telling you that some things — *most* things — can be talked through. Call your sisters, Gayle. Call Jack. None of this is a deal-breaker. You all love each other and want the best for one another. So make it right."

She drained the last of her cocktail and stood.

"Now, I'm all talked out and I need to get this tired old girl home."

Pixie stood with a groan and wagged her tail.

Gayle reached out and gave Jo's hand a final squeeze.

"See you tomorrow?" Jo asked.

Gayle nodded. "Love you, Jo."

"You too, Beanpole," Jo said, reverting to the nickname she'd given Gayle years ago. She squeezed her hand and then turned away. "Come on, Pixie girl. Let's go home."

Gayle leaned on the bar, her head spinning. Jo had bared her soul tonight. And as much as Gayle wanted to pretend that Jo's story had nothing to do with what was going on between her and her siblings, she knew it as a lie. At the end of the day, Jo was right. Was this the hill she wanted to die on? Was she prepared to lose some of the most important people in her life in order to protect the memory of the one she'd lost?

She thought of her sisters... the ones she knew and loved. The one she didn't know at all.

And something inside her shifted, almost like an old key in a rusty lock that finally gave.

"You're the big sister. It's time to grow up."

Jo was right. It was time to focus on the family she had left.

It was time to focus on the living.

13

LENA

LENA MILLED AROUND THE KITCHEN, contemplating a second cup of coffee. She'd already had one, but it had been a fitful night. After she'd gotten home, it had taken hours to settle in. She'd felt wired and confused and out of sorts. And once she had finally been able to go to sleep, her dreams had been just as disconcerting.

But also fun, if she was being honest with herself. Fun and a whole host of other adjectives. All of the good had fallen away in the light of day, though, and she just felt *shook*.

She had been down this road before, the constant dreams of Owen. They were especially bad whenever he traveled for months at a time and the daily, fraternal reality of her best friend was replaced by the unsettling fantasies of an overactive imagination.

She had laid them to rest years ago.

Mostly.

But they always resurfaced at the most unsettling times. Even more unsettling than the erotic dreams were the sweet and simple ones. Waking up together, staring into those sea-blue eyes. The two of them decades from now, white-haired and wrinkled, sitting on the wraparound porch of a butter-yellow house in a pair of rockers looking out at the sea.

The dreams were more than just narratives. What always stayed with her were the emotions that came with them. The sense of deep contentment and connection... of being perfectly and completely happy just to be there with him.

Last night was...not that. Last night was straight-up dirty dancing. The horizontal kind.

This morning, she had even gone so far as to take down the pictures of them on her fridge — each one showed the two of them in front of some scenic vista, looking for all the world like a couple in love — because whenever she got a glimpse of his stupid-gorgeous face, all the details from her dreams the night before came rushing back in.

She let out a low groan.

"Get out of my head!"

There had been a time when she would have let herself go back to bed and wallow, alternately aching for him and luxuriating in the fantasy of that *Twilight Zone* version of Owen who was head over heels in love with her.

But that was just a fantasy — because the hard truth was that Owen had had countless opportunities to make a move over the past three-plus decades, and he never had.

The truth hurt.

She needed to get her head on straight and not jeopardize their friendship by mooning over him. He was her dearest friend, and she had nearly pushed him away decades ago in her adolescent belief that if he couldn't be her boyfriend, he couldn't be her friend either. He had gone away for the summer and they'd had no contact at all, but then he had swaggered back into town full of stories, completely unaffected by their months of zero contact, acting like their friendship could resume as if there had been no pause at all...

And it had.

But the memory stayed with her. Owen loved her as a friend, but he wasn't *in* love with her. He didn't *need* her. And he never would. Not the way she'd dreamed of.

No. Whatever last night had been—her damned imagination again, or the allure of that stupid red dress—it wasn't real. Reading too much into what had happened would only drive her crazy. Nothing *had* happened, for Pete's sake, and already she felt unhinged.

A knock sounded at her front door and Lena raced towards it, relieved for the distraction of another person. She was so happy, in fact, that she forgot to feel awkward about seeing Anna alone for the first time. Lena greeted her sister with a hug.

"Oh, um, hello to you, too!" Anna said, squeezing her back with one arm. "Mind the food!"

Lena pulled back to see a slightly crumpled pastry box.

"Oh, you didn't need to do that," she said.

"I didn't!" Anna told her. "Nikki was up half the night baking for her interview today — they only asked her to make some entrees and appetizers, but she wanted to show off her dessert skills, too — and she left us everything that was slightly imperfect. There's basically no difference between dessert and a decadent breakfast, right?"

The three of them had planned to go to brunch, but Nikki had to bow out the night before because she had gotten a call from the owner of the new restaurant that was opening on the river. Diane wanted her to come in and cook some sample items for her and her investor partners. Nikki was a bundle of nerves, but Lena was confident that her sister would get the job. Her cooking was phenomenal, and she was sure to wow them. Farm to table got a little more complicated in Maine in the wintertime, but Nikki was a native. She knew plenty of farmers and townies who put things up hundreds of jars at a time. She was going to knock this one out of the park.

So that had left just Lena and Anna for Sunday Funday. Nothing in Lena's life was feeling particularly fun at the moment, but Anna was the sort of person who could always liven things up.

Lena smiled, taking the box from Anna. "The main difference is that at breakfast, I can balance it out with all the coffee I like and still sleep that night." If she could stave off those infernal Owen dreams, at least... "Come on through to the kitchen. I'll brew us a fresh pot."

"Those paintings are gorgeous," Anna said as they walked through the living room.

"Yeah, that's Freddie at his best. He gave me those three as a combo birthday-Christmas present years ago."

"Oh, is your birthday in December?"

"Nope. It's in May," Lena snorted, "but he realized that I had been working for him for years and had never had a birthday."

"Well that's... nice?"

"He never did bother to ask when my birthday was." Lena rinsed out her coffee filter and started another batch. "To be fair, he probably could have sold those for close to ten grand, at the time. So I guess it's worth quite a few years' worth of holidays. And I do love them."

Anna was still in the living room, staring at the paintings.

"It's like I'm seeing half a dozen things at once," she said, entranced. "Alternate realities all coexisting, layered on top of each other. The longer I look, the more I see. And it looked like an abstract, at first glance."

"They're something else," Lena said. Belatedly, she realized that this was Anna's first time at her house. She was off her game today. "Can I give you a tour while the coffee brews?" she asked.

"Please," Anna replied.

"Living room, kitchen, bathroom," Lena said carelessly, gesturing to each. "Come see the ballet studio."

Anna laughed in surprise. "The what?"

"The woman who sold me this house was a ballet teacher, and this was her studio." Lena opened a door off of her living room and led Anna into a massive room filled with art and light. "All I really did was take down the mirrors and bars. And collect things, over the years."

"This is extraordinary," Anna breathed. She gravitated towards a series of photographs, antique photos of Cherry Blossom Point before there was anything here that could really be called a town. Anna studied them for a long moment before moving on to a birdfeeder that hung from the ceiling.

I never should have walked into this room today, Lena thought. Everything in here reminded her of Owen.

"What's with the indoor bird feeder? Is it an art-out-of-place piece?" Anna joked. "Like when they put that toilet in the center of the MET?"

"Nothing so avant garde," Lena said with a wave of her

hand. "It just hangs in here during wintertime to keep it safe."

The bird feeder was actually one of Owen's early vases. She had swiped it and gotten a local metal worker to turn it into a hummingbird feeder. It had been her gift to him the year his mother had died. Hummingbirds had been his mom's favorite, and now there were always hummingbirds outside his kitchen window, May through September. It was so dear to him that he put it in what he called 'Lena's private art gallery' each year to keep it safe through the winter months... along with the rest of his favorite pieces, the ones that he couldn't bear to put in storage or risk smashing in his already crowded-with-pieces cottage.

The center of the room held a long table covered almost entirely in glasswork. Dusting it was a nightmare.

"These are all made by the same artist, yes? Your Owen?"

"Not *my* Owen," Lena corrected. "But yes."

Anna cocked an eyebrow at her but said not a word. She turned to regard a stained glass piece that hung in front of the windows. It featured a tyrannosaurus rex fleeing an erupting volcano. A pteranodon flew overhead.

"This is pretty much the coolest thing I've ever seen. And I get around."

Lena moved to stand beside her and smiled at the piece.

"It was meant to be a real window. Someone commissioned it for their house and then decided to do something different, but this was already paid for. I loved it so much that Owen wrapped it up and called it a birthday gift. I keep meaning to have it installed in the house. It's meant to be a real window, not just hang here like this."

Anna turned back to the table. "These vases are so

gorgeous. Does he have any for sale now? I'd love to bring some back to Bluebird Bay for Steph and Cee-cee."

"There were none at this showing, but I'm sure he has some in storage somewhere. So much of his best stuff just languishes in storage... or ends up here. We really need to get more eyes on his work."

She shot Anna a glance as an idea began to gel in her mind. She was working on a professional website for Owen. It was meant to be done by Christmas so that she could surprise him with it as a gift, but the pictures that she had taken with her old digital camera were subpar.

"I don't suppose... I know that you normally do nature photography, but if you're looking for some work while you're here, I'd love to hire you to take some photos of his work to put up on his website—"

"Sure," Anna said cheerfully. "I wanted to stop on my way here and get some shots of the frost on the windows of the chapel, so I have my camera in the car already. We can head over to the gallery after breakfast, if you'd like."

"Today?" Lena's stomach bottomed out as she thought of returning to the scene of the crime so soon. No, that was ridiculous. Nothing even *happened*, she reminded herself tersely.

"Why not?" Anna said with a shrug. "Nikki's tied up, and I've got nothing else to do. Taking a picture of pretty things that aren't flying away or trying to eat me sounds like a piece of cake."

"Thanks," Lena laughed. "Deal."

"But I'm not letting you pay me. Lucky for you, my fee has already been paid in pastries." Anna walked back towards the kitchen, saying over her shoulder, "And you can tip me in coffee."

"I'll tip you in coffee and whichever pieces from that table you'd like to bring home for Christmas," Lena said firmly. Nothing on the table was particularly dear to her. The pieces that had been made for her were scattered around her house, in daily use. An ornate bowl full of apples, candlesticks streaked with wax, ornaments hanging in her bedroom... those probably didn't help with the disturbing dreams, come to think of it.

No, don't think of it. Think of anything else.

"How was your hike with Dad the other day, by the way?" she asked as they sat down to coffee and dessert-for-breakfast.

"It was great. A love of nature and a fascination with wildlife are great things to have in common. It made for an easy outing." She paused to eat a bite of cheesecake. "Things got a little weird when we got back to town, though."

"Weird how?"

"We stopped for hot chocolate, and an older lady thought I was Nikki. When she realized her mistake, Eric introduced me as his daughter. She was... surprised."

"Oh." Tears sprang to Lena's eyes. She wasn't distressed, just moved. Eric loved his children so much. It must have been unutterably painful to have another child he was never allowed to see. And now to be able to spend time with her, to claim her.

How could the twins begrudge him that?

Lena cleared her throat. "That must have been Frannie. She's a sweetheart. We've all known her since we were kids. I'm sure she didn't mean anything by it. It's just... it is a little spooky, how much you and Nikki resemble each other."

Anna was quiet for a moment as she took a bite of the chocolate lava cake that Lena was eating. It was cold, and the center was solid chocolate ganache, but it was even more delicious that way. No chocolate wasted on the plate.

"Do you," Anna began, and then cut herself off emphatically, "*You*, Lena, not Gayle or Nikki or anyone else but you." She took a deep breath. "Do you think it would be better if I stayed away?"

"No!" Lena said reflexively. "Please, Dad would be crushed. And I'm just getting to know you. Don't let the twins run you off."

"That's sweet." Anna grinned. "But sorry, that's not what I meant. I don't scare that easy. I meant, do you think I should stay out of Cherry Blossom Point and just let Eric visit me in Bluebird Bay? Or, I don't know, meet in between for hikes? This is your home, and I know that my being here is going to kick up some dust."

Lena took a minute to consider her answer this time. She took a bite of chocolate ganache and let it melt in her mouth. She could taste sea salt, and a faint hint of orange. Nikki was going to get this job, no doubt.

"No," she said again.

"Why not?"

"Honestly?" she asked, eyeing Anna.

"Always."

"Because you were Dad's dirty secret long enough," Lena told her. Anna winced, and Lena pushed on. "He wants you here. It might not always be easy, but the best things never are. He wanted to bring you into the light because he loves you. He's proud of you. Now you just have to decide what *you* want."

Anna stared at her for a long moment and then nodded. "Okay. I'll do that."

When they had eaten all they could of Nikki's treats – which was roughly half of what she had sent – Anna grabbed her camera from her car and took pictures of each of the glass pieces in Lena's studio. Then, they got in Lena's car and went over to the gallery. They were closed on Sundays in the off-season, but Sheree used that time to set up new displays and do the books. Lena tapped on one of the front windows until Sheree appeared from the back room.

"Back so soon?" she greeted Lena with a smile as she opened the front door.

"We were hoping to take some pictures of Owen's things for his website. This is—" Lena hesitated for a fraction of a second before plunging forward, "my sister, Anna."

"Hey Anna, nice to meet you. Come on in," Sheree said agreeably. "Too bad you didn't get to take them before the opening. He sold a ton last night, and a lot of the buyers took the pieces home. They're small enough."

Lena frowned and surveyed the remaining pieces.

"That's all right. There are still a few of each for the website I'm making him. All we need is a good representation of the types of pieces he can create and then people can order in their preferred colors and such, if they want. We can work on building up his online portfolio over time."

"Have at it. I'll be in back. Just let me know when you're ready to head out so I can lock up after you."

"You've got it. Thanks."

Anna uncapped her camera and started snapping away. "This shouldn't take long."

"Thank you." Lena gravitated toward the green ornament she loved so much and frowned when she saw the sold sticker on the back. Maybe she'd ask Owen to—

"Fancy meeting you here," said a familiar brogue.

Crap.

She was so not ready to face him yet.

"Couldn't stay away?" Owen teased as he set down a large wooden crate. "And what's this one doing, then? Good to see you again, Anna."

"And you." Anna grinned at him, glanced at Lena, and went back to work.

"She's taking pictures, duh," Lena said, trying to keep her tone light despite the pandemonium going on in her body.

"Ah, I see. I'd never have guessed." He bent and began to empty the crate in a flurry of newspaper, setting new pieces on the table in a haphazard arrangement. "Well then, good news. Rather than taking photos of all the picked over stuff, I've brought some other things to fill in the gaps. If you'd like to wait a sec, I can display them?"

"Please," Lena said.

He lifted a stunning yellow vase from the box, and Anna instantly leaned toward it.

"That's mine. Is there another?"

"In storage there is," Owen chuckled. One of his globular ornaments rolled off of the table, and he snatched it just before it hit the marble floor. Lena moved forward and instinctively began arranging the pieces safely on the table, hanging the ornaments on the mostly-empty display. It was hard to concentrate with Owen next to her, radiating heat and smelling like man and woods and so yummy—

"That's enough photos," she said to Anna, her tone breathy and a little shrill. "We should leave now. Don't want to be late for the...thing."

"Right," Anna said with a sage nod, not missing a beat. "Want to get good seats for the thing. See you, Owen." She capped her camera and made for the coat rack.

"Lena," Owen began, leaning towards her. "I-"

"Sorry! Call you later, all right?" she said, stepping back. "The, um, the new pieces are great but I've gotta run. See you...soon."

With that, she turned and literally ran out the door.

When she climbed into the car on trembling legs, she found Anna there cracking up.

"So what was it you were saying? He's not *your* Owen? Because he sure seems like yours..."

She popped the car into drive and spared Anna a quick death stare that only had her laughing harder.

Lena didn't see any humor in any of it. She needed to rein in her feelings, and fast. As bad as she was at hiding them, it was only a matter of time before he figured it out, which would ruin everything.

The sooner things with Owen went back to normal, the better.

14

ANNA

ANNA SET her bags out on Nikki's dining table, admiring the Christmas presents. The vase was beautiful, a blending of soft to vibrant yellows that would look wonderful in her sister Cee-cee's apartment. Lena had also let her have a serving platter that featured a gorgeous painting of a sea turtle half covered by a blue glass glaze. That one was for her sister Stephanie. Steph had rescued a sea turtle with a broken shell the year before. She'd repaired the shell and even commissioned a pool where he could rehabilitate until he was strong enough to return to the wild. Steph had such a huge heart... just like her son Todd, who had taken over the veterinary practice as Steph transitioned slowly into retirement.

Anna felt a wave of homesickness, thinking of her family in Bluebird Bay. It was an unfamiliar feeling for such a short time away, something that she'd rarely suffered from all those years that she'd spent flying around the world doing nature photography. But she'd gotten used to having her sisters around all the time and seeing her family almost every day.

They had been texting daily since she left, but that wasn't the same.

What's happening? she sent on the text thread that included both of her Sullivan sisters.

Not much, what's happening there? Stephanie replied.

Missing you guys. Are you busy?

Just got back from class, Steph wrote. *FaceTime?*

Yes please!

Wait, Cee-cee chimed in. *Me too! Let's get on Skype. I'm just out walking Tilly. Be home in five.*

Anna put on a fresh pot of coffee and set her laptop up at the dining table. A call came in just as she was sitting down with her mug. She answered and Steph appeared, still wearing her yoga clothes and a high ponytail.

"Hi Steph!" Anna said. "I miss your face!"

"Well, it's about time the tables have turned," Steph laughed, "after all those years of me missing your face."

"Are you saying you don't miss my face now?" Anna demanded.

"I *see* your face now. The wonders of technology."

The screen split into three boxes, and Cee-cee's face appeared. Anna gasped.

"Cee-cee, your hair!" She had cut her long, dark locks into a honey-streaked bob that fell just above her chin.

Cee-cee wrinkled her nose and patted her bob with one hand. "You hate it?"

"I love it!" Anna exclaimed. "You look gorgeous. I'm only shocked that I wasn't consulted," she teased.

"It was a spur of the moment decision. I got tired of tying it up every day to bake, so I thought I'd try something shorter."

"It looks amazing. How's the shop?"

"Busy," Cee-cee said happily. "Between holiday cupcakes and the new savory line we've put out, I can hardly keep up. I hired another employee for the main location, and I'll probably need to hire a fourth in January."

"That's amazing."

"Wait til you taste these new savory cupcakes," Stephanie said. "There's this Italian sausage one that's just to die for. It's like a biscuit with cheese and meat... I can't even do it justice, but it's so good."

"How are the kids?"

"Can we even call them that anymore?" Cee-cee laughed. "Sasha and Gabe are good. I think Sasha is getting antsy already and she's still got another twelve weeks. Max is good; she and Ian are both really busy with work. All's well."

"Jeff's doing really well," Steph chimed in with a wide grin that lit up her face. "Mick's so impressed with his carpentry skills that this is looking less like a break from college and more like a viable career."

"And how do you feel about that?" Anna asked Stephanie. She had always assumed that all three of her kids would graduate from college, but her youngest had dropped out without telling her, not long after his dad died.

"As long as he's happy," Stephanie said. "I love that he's working with Mick, and I love having him home. Though lately he's been talking about finding his own place. He wants me to cosign on a loan so that he can buy a fixer-upper and flip it. Wait until you see the work he's done on the house! The kid eats and breathes carpentry these days. When he's not working with Mick, he's working at home. His video games are gathering dust. Cee-cee's right. None of them are kids anymore."

"They'll always be *your* kids," Anna insisted, "and I will not relinquish the right to refer to them as such. Not now, and not when they're fifty. I mean, really. You both still call me kiddo!"

"Touché," Steph laughed.

"How's Todd? He and Alice still doing good?" Her nephew's Thanksgiving date had fit into the Sullivan family celebration just as easily as Nikki and Beth had, utterly charming all of them.

"He's great, and they are," Steph said happily. "Her aunt is coming home soon, and Alice has moved into her house. Jeff's working on a wheelchair ramp for the front porch. I actually just saw them last night. Alice was playing her first local gig down at the bar. She plays fiddle and she's amazing. Anyway, they're good. Todd got one of his friends from school to move to Bluebird Bay so that they could share hours at the clinic. Clients are still pouring in through that website he built, and he just couldn't keep up. And once he met Alice, he actually *wanted* to make time for a life outside of work. He's working much more reasonable hours now."

"I'm glad. I know you were worried about him for a minute there."

"Well, that's what we do. We worry."

"Speaking of which," Cee-cee said, "how are things in Cherry Blossom Point?"

"Wonderful terrible," Anna said with a shrug. "I can give you all the gory details when I'm home eating those muffins I've been promised, but basically it's been half good, half bad.

Getting to know Eric has been lovely. No one will ever replace Pop's place in my heart, but Eric is like... this amazing uncle I never had, you know? And Lena's adorable. You'll love her. Maybe by the time you meet her she'll have finally admitted that she's crazy in love with this Irish hunk who follows her around like a puppy... I'm dying to say something, but I don't think I've earned the right to be quite that nosy yet."

"Ah, yeah. That takes some time, but you'll get there," Steph said with a chuckle. "And how are things with the Axis of Evil?"

"Not so loud," Anna shushed her, glancing around like she was afraid of getting caught. "That code name is top secret. But yeah, that's the bad half of the trip so far. I went to a family meeting at Gayle's bar and there was some contention about whether I should be there or not. She and Jack were both pissed off. Neither of them have spoken to me or any of their other family since. I hate that it's causing a rift. The last thing I want is to cause more stress for Lena and Nikki."

"Can I remind you of the advice you gave me once?" Cee-cee asked.

"No," Anna shot back reflexively.

"You can't fix everything for everyone."

"I don't appreciate my words being weaponized against me," Anna said, laughing.

"I'm just saying," Cee-cee started, and Anna interrupted her.

"What's that? I can't hear you. You're breaking up! I'm going through a tunnel."

Steph cackled and Cee-cee said, "You're in a house!"

"What? Can you still hear me?" Anna called, slowly closing her laptop. "Love you guys!"

"Love you, too!"

She clicked the laptop shut and bit back a smile. That was just what she'd needed. A moment to connect and see them. While she knew she was doing the right thing spending time with Eric, Lena, and Nikki, she still wasn't sure whether she was going about it the best way. She thought back to the question Lena had posed earlier.

Did she need to be in Cherry Blossom Point?

Before she could sink her teeth into that conundrum, her phone chimed and she opened a text from Beckett. There was a video attached, and Anna hit play.

"Say hi to Anna!" Beckett said from off screen.

"Hi Nana!" his grandson shouted. He was in the hallway of Beckett's house, sitting on a tiny strider bike.

"Show her what you can do."

Teddy propelled himself forward with bare feet, lifting them off the ground as the bike zoomed down the hallway. The camera phone shook as Beckett caught him, and Anna got a close-up of Teddy's smiling face before Beckett turned the screen around.

"He found the Christmas present that I'd hidden in the closet," Beckett said with a smile. "Who was I to deny him? That's it. Call me tonight?"

Anna watched the video a second time, laughing at the huge grin on Teddy's face. She couldn't help but wonder if Eric would love Beckett's baby grandson as much as she did... and realized with a start how much she cared about her father already.

There was no denying it. He was family.

She was sorry for the stress it was causing the twins, but she *did* want to be here. For the first time since leaving Bluebird Bay, she felt at peace with her choice. And not only that, but Eric, Nikki, and Lena wanted her here too. So here she would stay. For a while longer. If they wanted to come up to Bluebird Bay for a stay at some point next year... well, that sounded good too.

Anna's stomach rumbled, and she went into the kitchen to rummage through the decadent leftovers in Nikki's fridge. The front door opened and shut, and Nikki came straight into the kitchen, looking nervous and excited.

"How'd it go?" Anna asked her.

"I think they liked me. I don't know. The owner was kind of a closed book. But everything went well, no disasters, even though it was my first time in that kitchen. It's a *nice* kitchen. State of the art."

"You're an amazing chef, Nikki. You've got this."

"I hope so. I can't coast too much longer on my savings before going back to my old job. I *liked* that job, but the hours there would make it really tough to go back and forth between here and Mateo's place. I could at least wait until January without depleting my savings too badly, which would give us some long weekends together before I need to work around a restaurant schedule. I have some money set aside, but I wouldn't want to cut it too close. Beth's scholarships pay her tuition but there's still rent and food and books and I don't want her to have to take out loans—"

"Nikki," Anna interrupted. "Take a breath. It's going to be great. You've got this job, I just know it."

Nikki took a deep breath and nodded. "Yeah. Yeah, okay. I have to stay positive."

Her phone rang and she yanked it from her purse, nearly fumbling it in her excitement. Her eyes went wide as she stared down at the screen and she hit the green button to answer.

"Hello?"

A second later, she turned to Anna and held the phone out at arm's length.

"It's for you."

Anna frowned at her. Who would be calling on Nikki's phone? Even Eric had her number...

"It's Gayle."

15

LENA

IT HAD BEEN A REALLY nice day with Anna, she thought as she nudged the fridge door closed with her hip.

So then why did you order a small pizza, eat the whole thing, and then head straight for the freezer for some Chocolate Chip Cookie Dough ice cream?

"Mind your own business," she muttered to her subconscious as she set her bowl on the table and topped it off with whipped cream.

There was no getting around it. She was stress eating, and she knew just who to blame.

She let out a groan and plugged a spoonful of the creamy concoction into her mouth.

Owen. Why was he putting her through this? It probably wasn't even intentional. *Maybe as he got older, all that sexy got even harder to contain and just started oozing out,* she mused with a sigh.

After eating her dessert and watching babies do funny things on TikTok for a while, she was feeling marginally less sorry for herself. Maybe a long read in a hot bubble bath before bed would be just the ticket, and she'd actually get some decent sleep tonight.

She dumped her dirty bowl in the sink and headed into the master bathroom, stripping her clothes off as she went. For the next hour, she soaked in a tub of heady lavender bubbles, doing her darndest not to think of You Know Who.

She'd almost managed it, and she had her nose buried in a brand new thriller she'd been saving for an emergency when her phone rang.

She shot it a scowl from across the room and ignored it... but twenty seconds later, it rang again.

Maybe Gayle had decided to open the lines of communication again.

And maybe you should just keep ignoring that phone, a little voice chimed in. She'd reached her capacity for stress today. But when it started ringing a third time, fear crept in.

"Dang it," she muttered as she squirmed her way out of the tub. Quickly, she slung a towel around herself and padded across the tile floor on still-wet feet.

The phone stopped ringing a second before she answered, but the screen still displayed the name of her caller.

Owen.

It was so unlike him to be that persistent. If he needed her, normally he'd just text.

With shaking hands, she dialed him back.

He was okay. Surely he was okay...

"Hello?" she said cautiously as the phone stopped ringing. "Owen...is everything all right?"

There was a long silence on the other end, and Lena's heart dropped to her stomach.

"Jerry...Gemma's husband was just killed in a car wreck."

* * *

Lena parked outside of Owen's apartment thirty minutes later and sat in the car for a minute, steadying herself. She was gutted for Gemma and the kids, but right now she needed to be strong for Owen so that he could be strong for them.

Her mind flitted to his nephews and she blanched, remembering when her own were around that age. Death was so uncompromising...so unbearably final. No matter how much your mind tried to work the problem, to wheel and deal its way out of the pain, it stood its ground. Unyielding.

Ruthless.

She forced out a breath and shoved the car door open.

Owen lived in an old brick building that had been split into four living spaces. His apartment upstairs was tiny, but his space on the first floor was much bigger, perfect for his glass studio. He had lived there ever since he'd made the jump from working as a tattoo artist to becoming a full-time glassblower. It had been an insane pay cut, but that was Owen. Never money motivated. But not careless, either. He and Gemma owned the house where their parents had lived for twenty years, and owned it outright. They split the rent that they collected each month, and Owen's half went into a retirement fund.

On a hunch, Lena walked into the lower level instead of up the stairs. Owen was working on a large pitcher, wielding a metal pipe in one hand and a pair of tongs in the other. He was in the process of turning a blob of molten glass into a handle. Lena stood back, waiting until he was at a safe place to pause.

Suddenly, Owen lifted the pitcher into the air and slammed it against the floor. The body shattered, and the gooey handle stuck to the floor like a glob of gum. His shoulders shook.

"Owen?" Lena said hesitantly.

He jumped and turned around. "Lena! Sorry, I didn't see you there. Are you alright?"

"Are *you*?"

Owen shrugged and looked away. His eyes were red.

"Have you eaten yet today?"

"I haven't, and I don't plan to. Can't stomach it, frankly." Owen walked off, leaving the floor strewn with shards of glass. Lena made a mental note to clean it up before she left and then followed him up the stairs.

"Do you want a drink?" he asked as she walked in. Without waiting for an answer, he poured two tall glasses of whiskey over ice. Lena accepted hers and sipped carefully, while Owen practically gulped his down.

Owen was never much of a drinker. His father had been an alcoholic who had been sober from Owen's thirteenth birthday up to the day he died... which was far too young, due to liver disease. It had been a fate Owen refused to emulate. Lena had never seen him have more than one glass of whiskey or a couple of beers at a time.

"Do you want to talk about it?" she asked.

"I don't." Owen poured himself a second glass and went to sit on his couch. Lena followed, still nursing her first glass of whiskey. Owen sat with his shoulders hunched, eyes down, and Lena looked around the room. She usually avoided coming up here, partly because her house was bigger and made for a better hang out spot, but partly out of fear she might see some other woman's underwear on the floor or a second toothbrush in the bathroom.

It was a small studio, but it was beautiful. High ceilings and red brick walls, with one wall almost completely filled with windows. It was a corner apartment with two more windows on a second wall. One side looked out over the river, the other over their little town. She understood why he chose to make do with such a small space.

"It's bad, Lena," Owen said miserably. "She can't even get through a conversation without breaking down. They only got there two days ago. They were bringing the moving truck to the rental place. They were right there, Lena." His own voice broke as he said it, and Lena laid her hand on his arm. "When that damned truck hit the one Jerry was driving, they were just a few cars behind him. Gemma had to veer off the road."

"Oh no," Lena said. "Is she okay? Are the kids okay?"

"Physically, yeah. But God, Lena. Jerry was still alive when she got to him. She couldn't get him out of the van."

Lena brought a hand to her mouth, stifling a horrified sob.

"They're in some hotel in Massachusetts. The house was still in shambles, boxes everywhere, nothing unpacked. Jerry's folks are with them."

At least they weren't alone. "That's good."

"I'm glad they're there, but Lord. Imagine losing a child."

She'd seen it up close and personal, and bearing witness to that pain had been the most devastating thing she'd experienced in her lifetime.

"They're in no position to take care of her, but Gemma made me wait until morning before driving down. She was terrified of having me drive at night, after..."

"It's okay," Lena soothed. "It's just as well. This gives you a moment to pull yourself together so you can really be there for her and the kids."

"You know Jerry arranged our mam's funeral?" More tears fell down Owen's face, but his voice was steady. "Gemma and I were too broken-hearted, the both of us. He took care of everything."

"It was a beautiful service," Lena said as Owen poured himself another glass of whiskey. "Are you sure I can't make you something? Eggs?"

"You know they met in college?" Owen asked, ignoring her question and slumping back onto the couch. "They were friends for years before he worked up the courage to make a move. Friends first. Gemma always swore by it, said she couldn't imagine going about it any other way."

He took another long drink of whiskey.

"I never got to know him as well as I would've liked, them living all the way out in Denver. But I visited enough to know he was a good man...a good father to those kids. Those poor boys." Owen's voice was so hoarse, she could hardly hear him now.

"I know," Lena murmured, wishing like hell she could take his pain away.

"She'll move here," Owen slurred. She wondered if he had started drinking before she'd gotten here or if it was just the effect of an empty stomach and low tolerance for alcohol. "She has to, now. Move here. Move home. She can live in Mam's house for free. Why wouldn't she?"

"Give her some time," Lena said. "Don't push her to make a decision now. I think the best thing that you can do is be there for the kids, give her space to grieve."

"Ah, damn it," Owen groaned. He set his empty glass down on the table and put his face in his hands. "My heart is breaking for those boys."

Lena rubbed his shoulder and they were quiet for a time.

"Let me make you something to eat," she coaxed. "At least some toast."

"Yeah," he acquiesced. "Okay."

Lena found a sourdough loaf in the fridge and cut two generous slices. Something to sop up the whiskey, if it wasn't all in his bloodstream already. She toasted the bread and added a bit of butter and marmalade, Owen's favorite combination.

"You're a saint," he said as she set the plate down in front of him. He'd gotten himself another glass of Jameson while her back was turned. She drank the last of her own, which was mostly water at this point. Owen took a bite of toast and chewed slowly.

"Remember when I taught you to drive stick-shift?" he asked.

Lena laughed in surprise. "What made you think of that?"

"That license plate there." He gestured to the old black-and-white plate that hung on the wall. *MAINE*, it read above the six-digit number. And below it, *VACATIONLAND*. He had laid his beloved Mustang to rest years ago, and the plate had hung on his wall ever since.

"I was terrified you were going to crash Delilah or burn the clutch out, but you were so determined. I couldn't say no. I could never say no to you."

That last claim held a strange intensity, as did his stormy eyes as he looked at her, and she glanced away.

"I almost forgot you called your car Delilah," she said with a nervous little laugh.

"Delilah was a real trooper. Always around when I needed her." Owen's voice was thick with reminiscence... and drink. "Remember when Billy Weimer stood you up, and I drove you to that dance?"

"He did not stand me up," she corrected with a fond grin. "He had mono."

"Whatever," Owen said agreeably, closing his eyes. "I can still see you in that dress. It was peach, covered in sparkles. Your shoulders were bare, and your hair was loose. A halo of curls, all around your head. Like an angel." He opened his eyes, and there was that same intensity to his gaze as before.

"I can't believe you remember the dress I wore."

"I remember more than you could ever imagine." He reached out and wound one of her curls around his finger, eyes intent on her hair. "Everything. You looked almost as good then as you did last night, in that red dress..."

"Owen," she began, her stomach diving to her toes. "I don't th—"

He cut her off with a kiss as he slanted his lips over hers. At first, she was frozen with shock, but soon enough, the scent of him, the warmth of him, the feel of him overwhelmed her. Lena's body responded without her permission, pressing closer. A soft groan escaped Owen's lips and he pulled her closer still, erasing the space between them. One hand slipped into her hair; the other cupped her cheek as he took the kiss deeper. For a short time, Lena's mind was completely, deliciously blank.

Then she smelled the whiskey on his breath.

No.

She dug deep and dragged herself away.

"Owen, no. You're not thinking straight." The man was grief-stricken—and drunk to boot. This wasn't real. He didn't mean it, and he'd be embarrassed in the morning... if he remembered this at all.

"I am," he murmured. "Lena—"

"I'll be back. I'm going to make you an egg sandwich," she interrupted, gently disentangling his hand from her curls. "You need some real food. Just... stay there," she ordered as she stood up from the couch.

"Why do you always push me away?" he muttered. She turned to look at him in surprise, and he said in a softer tone, "Don't run away from me, Lena. Please."

"I'm not running," she said, ducking behind the kitchen counter. "I'm making some food so you can function well enough to drive safe tomorrow." She opened the cabinet door in search of a pan and stayed there for a long moment, crouched behind the counter like a soldier sheltering from shrapnel.

She had to get it together, here.

All her life, she'd wondered what it would be like to kiss Owen McKenna. Now she knew, and she wished to God that she didn't. It was like nothing she had ever experienced, nothing she had ever imagined. No romantic encounter in her life had been as all-consuming as that kiss, blotting out the rest of the world. Even with the couple long-term boyfriends she'd had, there was always a shred of self-consciousness. Something that kept her from fully surrendering to the moment. Not with Owen, though. He always made her feel safe.

He's not safe, she thought vehemently. *He's the most*

dangerous man in the world. Now protect your heart and make some damned eggs.

So Lena did just that, breaking the yolks as she flipped them with a shaky hand. She put the eggs on toast, added a few shakes of tabasco, and walked back around the countertop to find Owen out cold. He was lying on his back, one hand resting on the floor.

If she'd been wondering whether maybe he'd been more sober than she thought (and knew what he was doing when he kissed her) she wondered no more.

Oof.

"You can't sleep like that, you big lug," Lena muttered to herself as she set the plate down on the coffee table. He might throw up and choke or something. That image helped to blot out the too-recent memory of his body pressing against hers...

Stop that.

She tried to roll him onto his side, but he wouldn't budge. He was too heavy. She sighed and sat down in the sliver of space that remained on the couch. She would have to watch over him until he'd slept it off some, and then she could get him into bed with some aspirin and water in him.

Just then, he rolled onto his side and kicked against the opposite arm of the couch, pushing his head up onto her thighs. With a weary sigh, he wormed one arm between the couch and Lena's lower back, and then sank back into a deep sleep.

Lena's heart was beating so fast that she could feel her pulse thrumming in her throat. She lifted a hand and paused, fingers hovering just above Owen's head, before she let herself brush his hair back. Then she took a slow breath.

This was totally normal. It was what people did when

death snatched someone away. They clung to the most stable thing at hand. And for Owen, that was her. Trusty, solid, dependable Lena.

She would do everything that she could for Owen in his time of need, which meant not letting him do something that he'd regret tomorrow.

She would also protect herself in the process and make sure he couldn't break her heart by accident...

Tomorrow.

Tonight, just for a moment, she would let her walls down.

She relaxed into the couch, ran a hand through Owen's hair, and let herself look at his beautiful face.

Just for a moment.

16

NIKKI

A WORRISOME MORNING called for steel-cut oats. It was simpler fare than the rest of the food Nikki had been cooking lately, but it was one of her favorite comfort foods. She loved to eat them with butter, maple syrup, and toasted walnuts—just like they had eaten on winter mornings growing up. On weekends, Dad would make pancakes, eggs, French toast...all sorts of stuff. Weekday mornings, it was boxed, cold cereal on repeat. But snow days?

Hot, sweet, delicious oats.

The past few days had been a flurry of food, really putting her kitchen to use. She had tested all sorts of new recipes, working with what she had been able to get last-minute from old friends. The farmers she always purchased her meat from were an easy green light, but she had wanted to wow Diane with a menu that was entirely local. So she had hit up local vendors and called in favors with friends and neighbors until her countertops were bustling with root-cellar veggies, colorful jars of fruit preserves, and frozen summer butter. She had even purchased stone-ground local flours for sourdough and cake, plus some Maine-grown split peas for soup. Everything she needed to wow the new restaurant.

It had taken a few tries to get her desserts just right, working with the stone-ground flour. But even the first results were good enough for her sisters, and the final batch was good enough for anybody. Cooking her entrées in a kitchen she had never seen before, that was the real test. But Nikki had been in enough restaurant kitchens to find her way around anywhere, and the test meals had gone off without a hitch.

Diane's face had been inscrutable... But the lines in her forehead had eased when she tasted Nikki's beef and lamb moussaka, and her companions had gone crazy for the fennel pâté on fresh sourdough. Nikki could almost swear that she had seen a glimmer of a smile on Diane's face when she took a bite of her sweet potato pumpkin gnocchi.

Diane had told her that she would call in the next day or two to let her know if she got the job, and Nikki had hardly slept. She had tried for a while, then given up and gone into the kitchen for a plate of first-try baked goods.

Her phone buzzed on the counter, and she nearly jumped out of her skin. She grabbed it and saw Diane's name, stunned that she was calling so soon.

That was either really bad news or really good news.

Deeeep breath, she coached herself.

"Hello?" she answered in a surprisingly normal voice.

"Hi Nikki. It's Diane. So...Can you start the week before Christmas?"

Nikki tried to reply, but her voice caught in her throat.

"The grand opening is New Year's Eve, but this would give you time to create a menu, get to know the staff—"

"I-I got the job?"

"You got the job," Diane said warmly. "Nikki, I can't tell you how grateful I am to have found someone with your talent at the last minute. When my cousin quit on me... well, I didn't know how I was going to be ready for opening night and find a chef who could do these local ingredients justice. But you did that and more. You made that food sing."

Nikki's heart was hammering in her chest. "Thank you," she managed.

"Come in on the thirteenth around noon. We'll have some contracts ready for you to sign. We'll work out a schedule then."

"Yes ma'am!"

Diane hung up and Nikki stood there for a long moment, the phone still pressed to her ear. She wanted to run in and wake up Anna, but she settled for texting Mateo and Beth.

I GOT THE JOB! Nikki threw in some celebration and food emojis for good measure.

The front door flew open and Lena rushed in.

"I got the job!" Nikki shouted immediately, and then paused. "Wait...What are you doing here?"

"Congratulations," Lena said with a shaky smile. "I knew you would."

She closed the door and tugged off her coat, tossing it onto a nearby armchair. It took a second to sink in through all the adrenaline, but her sister was a wrinkled mess, and her hair hadn't been brushed...

Nikki gasped and leaned out over the half wall that separated the living room from her kitchen.

"Did you just do the walk of shame to my house?" she stage-whispered.

"What?" Lena looked down with a start. "No! Well, not the way you think, anyway. I did sleep at Owen's..."

Her sister's voice was thick with tears and Nikki turned off her stovetop before rushing into the living room.

"What's wrong? What happened?"

"Jerry died." She sat on the couch and leaned back, letting her eyes close for a moment.

"Who?" Nikki asked, confused for a moment.

"Gemma's husband."

Horror shot through her, eclipsing her excitement. "No!"

"Yeah." Lena's eyes were still closed. She looked pale and exhausted.

"Stay there." Nikki gave her sister a quick kiss on the forehead. "I'll get you a cup of coffee."

She went to the kitchen and made her sister breakfast in a mug — coffee with cream and maple syrup and two heaping scoops of collagen protein — then grabbed her own coffee and took both back to the couch.

"Owen just found out yesterday," Lena said as Nikki settled in next to her. "He left first thing this morning for Massachusetts."

"I thought they lived in Colorado?"

"They did." Lena paused and took a long drink of coffee. "Thanks for this," she added with a shuddering sigh. "Anyway, Gemma had just taken a new job in Mass. Jerry was dropping the moving van off and got hit by a semi-truck. Gemma must be destroyed, but she has her two boys to take care of, and Jerry's parents met them at the hotel, but they must be just as wrecked. Owen's going down there to try to pick up the pieces, be there for the boys so that Gemma can take some space to fall apart and put herself back together again."

"Awful," Nikki said softly. "Poor Gemma. She's so sweet and lovely. What a tragedy."

She couldn't stop the tears that rushed to her eyes. For Gemma. For boys who had to grow up without their loving father. And, most of all, for Jerry's poor parents. If it had been her… if it had been Beth, Nikki would have lay down and died right then and there. Or tried to. No doubt Gayle would have picked her up and force-fed her until she regained the will to live, like they all had tried to do for Jack back when—

Don't think about it.

Nikki squeezed Lena's hand. "Thank God she has Owen."

"I know," Lena said quietly, and sighed. "I only met Jerry a few times. Once when he and Gemma were in town for their wedding. You know how wedding weekends are, there's hardly time to have a conversation with the people you *already* know. And then again when they came out for her parents' funerals. Other than that, he mostly stayed back to work when she and the boys came to visit. But what I do know is that he was a good husband and an amazing father. To have him snatched away just as they were starting their next chapter, just as those boys are about to grow into men… it's just too cruel."

For a long time, they sat there quietly as Lena sipped her coffee.

"So you got the job," she murmured eventually, trying for a smile and almost succeeding.

"I did," Nikki said with a nod as she released her sister's hand and made her way to the stove. "I'm really pleased."

It seemed trivial in the midst of all this, right now, though...

"Stop it," Lena said softly. "The world keeps spinning, Nik. You know that. You don't have to feel bad for being excited about a huge, life-changing event. It's so good. In fact, it's just the news I needed today. Have you called Dad yet?"

Nikki shook her head as she stirred the oats.

"Not yet. I literally got the call just a couple minutes before you got here."

"He's going to be so excited."

Nikki nodded as she made the rounds, coffee pot in hand, and topped off each of their cups before sitting down again. It was only then that she noted the dark circles under Lena's eyes, and the haunted expression that spoke of something more than just the faraway tragedy that had rocked Owen's family.

"What else is going on with you?" Nikki asked cautiously. "You don't look right."

"Nothing else," Lena replied. "I just didn't sleep. I was up all night, just sitting on Owen's couch."

"Okay." Nikki sipped her coffee, waiting for the rest of the story.

"He fell asleep in my lap," Lena mumbled.

And there it is.

Her sister cupped the coffee mug more tightly as she cleared her throat. "He was drunk. I've never seen him drink that much, not in the thirty years I've known him. Even as a kid, he was so careful. He'd seen what alcohol could do."

"And what did it do to him last night?" Nikki pressed.

"Nothing. I mean, well... almost nothing."

"Come on, Lena. Spill it," she murmured, knowing it wouldn't take long to pull it out of her.

"He... he kissed me," Lena admitted in a voice so low that it was almost a whisper.

"He what?" Nikki demanded. "On the lips?"

"Yes on the lips," Lena snapped back, looking alive for the first time since she walked in. "It meant nothing. He was grief-stricken and drunk."

"I've been both, and I never made out with anyone because of it," Nikki shot back.

Lena glared at her. "He doesn't even remember what he did. This morning he just thanked me for sitting with him, downed some black coffee, and hit the road."

"Mm-hm." Nikki leaned back and took another sip of coffee.

"Really, Nikki. We're just friends. We've always been friends. It just threw me for a loop is all. And in the scheme of things, it's nothing."

Nikki just looked at her sister, taking in her pink cheeks and obvious anxiety. It wasn't nothing. When was Lena going to admit to herself that she was in love with Owen? She always had been. Sure, she'd had boyfriends, but they were like warm glasses of milk on a summer's day. Not revolting and objectively terrible, like Nikki's Steve had been, but definitely not appealing. If Lena brought another bland placeholder to fill in Owen's rightful space in her life, Nikki might scream. But Lena could be almost as stubborn as Gayle when she wanted to be, and pushing her on the issue right now would only cause her to dig her high heels in deeper.

"Do you want some actual breakfast? I made oatmeal."

"Sure," Lena said with a shrug.

"Oh, hi," Anna said blearily as she shuffled through the living room. "Is there coffee?"

"Always," Nikki replied.

"Yaaay," Anna said in a long monotone. Nikki followed her into the kitchen and served up three bowls of oatmeal, adding liberal amounts of cream. She paused to check her phone — there was a voice message from Mateo and an all-caps text from Beth, both congratulating her on the new job. She made a mental note to call each of them, and her dad, after breakfast.

By the time they were sitting at the table, Anna was halfway through her first cup of coffee and looking something closer to human.

"I have an announcement to make," Nikki said, clinking her spoon against her coffee mug.

"You got the job?!" Anna exclaimed, perking up instantly.

"Hey!"

"What?" Anna shrugged. "Lucky guess. They'd be fools not to hire you. But congratulations. You deserve it."

"Thanks," Nikki said with a grin.

"By the way," she said, turning to Lena, "I finished editing those pictures I took of Owen's work. Do you want to see?"

"Yes please," Lena replied around a mouthful of oatmeal.

Thank God for Anna. This would be a great short-term distraction from the heavy weight of everything going on, which Lena clearly needed.

Anna padded back to her room and came back with her laptop.

"Have you told Gayle about the job yet, or are you still

being shunned too?" Lena asked quizzically as Anna opened the computer and booted it up.

"Actually, I'm not sure," Nikki replied with a chuckle. "But you'll never guess who's off the shunned list..."

Lena raised her brows and then gasped as Nikki shot a pointed glance at Anna.

"Wait, what?!"

"Yep. Gayle called yesterday and asked to talk to Anna. They are meeting up tonight at the Moonlight Diner after the bar closes so they can talk."

"Why so late?"

Anna shrugged. "She said she wanted to talk to me ASAP and in person but had a bunch of appointments during the day. I stay up late anyway, so..."

Lena's eyes narrowed and she nodded as she turned her attention back to Nikki. "Okay, so are we giving her the benefit of the doubt here, or are you and I going to be hiding behind some potted rubber trees in case she brings a weapon?"

Anna let out a guffaw. "Trust me, I can take Gayle if it comes to that."

Lena's eyes went wide as she shook her head. "You think that cuz she's skinny, but I swear, it's all rangy muscle."

"Did you know that Jack runs the local Self Defense Academy? I know for a fact, she can eviscerate a man with a set of car keys if she had to," Nikki added.

"If I see her lunge for the keys, I'll know it's about to go down," Anna said solemnly. "Honestly, if I was going just by her tone, I'd say she has some things she needs to get off her chest. Murder isn't on the menu. You two will be the first to know, though."

She clicked her mousepad and a grid of images filled the screen. For the next half hour, they scrolled through hundreds of pictures of Owen's work as they ate. There was the vase Anna had claimed, a gorgeous piece with a long neck and a delicately ruffled rim. Shots of his plates, each one a different color of ombre. The globes that he had made into Christmas ornaments, delicate swirls of color.

"This one's my favorite," Lena said as a platter appeared on the screen. Owen had painted an intricate octopus, suckers and all, and glassed over it in shades of blue and gray and green. Half of the orange octopus was underwater, and half of it was on a small section of the platter that was pure white.

"I keep telling him to incorporate more of his illustrations into his glasswork," she continued with a rueful shake of her head. "Those ones always sell so quick. This one only made it onto my wall because I snatched it up before the series went to the gallery. If he did more of the silk-screened glass, he could produce enough for the gift shops in town, too." She paused and started tapping on the keyboard. "Take a look at this, so far."

Owen's website came up, and Nikki was blown away at how professional it looked. The photos were so-so, but once Lena replaced them with the shots Anna had taken...

"This is going to look amazing," Anna said. "The website looks so professional, but also really personal and inviting."

Lena clicked over to the bio page to reveal photos of Owen working with globs of molten glass, his face lit by the light of his forge. These shots were much better... but the handsome Irishman made for a forgiving subject. There was a paragraph about Owen, an address for the gallery, and links to his social media pages.

"You could do this for a living," Nikki told Lena.

"What, design websites?" she replied with a laugh. "No way. It took me hours to figure out how to make this one."

"And now you know how. But no, not just the websites," Nikki explained. "Representing artists. Lena, you're squandering your talent just working for Freddie. You have such a great eye for art. You're so organized, and you've obviously got a knack for the tech side of things...I don't know exactly how it would all work, but there is an idea in there..."

Lena shook her head, but her expression was thoughtful.

"Imagine it. Ferreting out the next great artist instead of running ridiculous errands for Freddie all day long. Helping them showcase their work."

Lena closed the laptop with a snap. "I don't have the headspace for that right now."

"Fair enough," Nikki said. "Just think about it when you do, okay?"

Lena shook her head again, but Nikki had to hope that the seeds had been planted.

The man of her dreams, the job of her dreams... it was all right there in front of her.

If only Lena would reach out and take it.

17

ANNA

ANNA SAT in an empty booth at the Moonlight Diner, scanning the plastic menu for the third time around.

"Did you want to wait for your companion to order or...?" the waitress asked with a kind smile.

Anna spared a glance at the young woman's name tag. Clearly "Leah" thought Anna had been stood up. And maybe she had. It was nearly eleven thirty, so either Gayle had gotten caught up and was running late, or she'd had a change of heart. Anna wouldn't have been surprised either way. It was a big step. Then again, Gayle had set their meeting place in a town neighboring Cherry Blossom Point at 11 PM, so maybe it wasn't a step at all. Maybe she just wanted to warn Anna, one on one, up close and personal, to back off.

Anna sighed, wishing she could fast forward to the next day and put an end to this nauseating combination of anticipation and dread.

"I'll just have a cup of decaf and a slice of apple pie," she said with a tight smile.

Whether she would eat it here or take it to go remained to

be seen.

"Great, I'll be right back with that."

Leah headed off to put her order in just as the bell on the door jangled. Anna looked up to find Gayle stepping into the diner, her expression carefully blank. There were only two tables with patrons at them, and her gaze collided with Anna's almost immediately.

As Gayle stalked toward her, the theme song from the movie *Jaws* began to play in Anna's head, keeping time with the older woman's strides.

"I apologize for being late. We had a discrepancy with the register, and it took some time to untangle," Gayle said, tugging off her black wool coat and laying it carefully on the seat before sliding in after it.

"It's fine," Anna began, but Gayle cut her short.

"It's not fine. I wasted your time. I don't like wasting people's time."

Anna shrugged, at a loss as to how to respond to that. She was fairly sure only Gayle Merrill possessed the skill to apologize in a way that made the other person feel like they'd done something wrong. "Alrighty then..." Anna said.

Thankfully, their waitress came back to take Gayle's order, diffusing the awkward moment.

"Just chamomile tea for me."

Leah slipped away, leaving Anna and Gayle to square off like a pair of boxers.

"Look, Gayle—"

"Anna, I—"

They both broke off and paused.

"I'll go first," Gayle said with a sigh. "I know we got off on the wrong foot the other day, and I also know that's partially my fault." She held up a single finger and shook her head. "Correction. It's mostly my fault. So, looks like tonight is going to be full of apologies on my part. I was angry at Nikki, and I took that out on you. Or, at the very least, certainly didn't treat you in a respectful way. I'm sorry for that."

Anna studied her older half-sister's face and realized with a start that she was actually quite beautiful. She'd heard so much about her, and the icy vibe she'd been giving off was so all-encompassing the first time they'd met, she hadn't realized. But with her thick, almost-black locks and wide dark eyes, she was quite the stunner. Even the fine lines on her face only seemed to make her look more earthy and real. Like a movie star who'd decided to give the plastic surgeon a pass.

"Well, if it helps any, I get it. I really struggled when I found out about my mom and all. For weeks, I raged at the world. I fought with my sisters because they were urging me to give Nikki a chance, and I felt so betrayed." She paused as Leah delivered their drinks and her pie before melting away. "Anyway, it goes without saying that of course I forgive you. In fact, I was never mad at you in the first place."

At least, not about that...

A smile quirked the corner of Gayle's mouth. "You seemed pretty pissed when I told Nikki off."

Anna nodded and took a sip of her coffee. "Yeah, well, I was always the little sister before Nikki came around. The big sister instinct kicked in really fast. In hindsight, I realize how presumptuous that must've seemed to you."

Gayle traced a finger around the rim of her steaming mug and fixed her gaze on a spot over Anna's shoulder. "That wasn't what set me off. I think... I guess, I just hate feeling misunderstood."

It was such a self-aware, vulnerable thing to say that for a second, Anna was taken aback. It seemed off-brand for the Gayle she'd heard so much about.

"I think most people can relate to that. I know I can."

"Yeah... but for me, it's sort of my legacy. One I've earned, to some degree, I guess. There are things I've done...and do, that I thought my sisters understood. I always had my reasons, right or wrong, and I was under the impression that they knew what they were. It just hit me that I was way off base. They think I'm mean. Jack too. You know they call us the Axis of Evil behind our backs?" Her lips twitched into a half-smile as if she got the humor, but it faded fast. "They think we are just on the hunt for things to scold them about, and that we don't care if we hurt their feelings in the process." Gayle shook her head and took a sip of her tea before meeting Anna's gaze. "The truth is, aside from my kids, those two women are my heart and soul."

Anna didn't know her well, but she knew the truth when she heard it. Compelled, she leaned in closer.

"So why are you so hard on them?"

"From an outside perspective, it must seem like I flew out of the womb on a broom or something. There is so much history here, though." She let out a long sigh. "You already know Jack and I are the oldest. When Lena was born, she had some issues that led to juvenile asthma. She was such a sickly baby. It resolved itself by the time she reached her teens, which happens with asthma sometimes, but there were very scary points." She bit her lip and paused for a second to collect herself. "It was up to the whole family to keep an eye on her to make sure she didn't overexert herself when we were playing and things like that. You only have to see a toddler gasping and wheezing, wide-eyed and panicked, one time for it to stick in your mind forever," she said, shifting in her seat. "It's so funny because Lena never thinks about it anymore, and Nikki barely remembers it because she was so small. But Jack and I remember. It made us very protective of her, and that watchfulness trickled down to Nikki. As Lena became an adult, we tried to let the reins go some, but then Nikki had a tough run of it in her late teens. She had self-esteem issues and made some bad choices in boyfriends, culminating with Steve."

Anna shivered at the memory of Steve, which was all too fresh.

"One minute, he was just another jerk with a god complex... the next, he was controlling who she saw and where she went. We knew he was bad for her."

A lump formed in Anna's throat and she resisted the urge to reach out and take Gayle's hand.

"But in the midst of all this, Jack's son River... he, um..." Gayle reached a shaking hand out and snatched a napkin from the dispenser, using it to swipe at her teary eyes. "He died on a fishing trip with Jack. From carbon monoxide poisoning. It was like our family was hit by a wrecking ball. He was just a little boy, eight years old, and I swear, I wasn't sure we were going to survive it."

Fat tears plopped from Anna's chin onto the table and she sucked in a steadying breath.

"I'm so, so sorry, Gayle," she managed, but the words felt hollow. What could she possibly say or do to even touch on that kind of pain?

"It was a terrible time," Gayle admitted with a nod. "But I'm not telling you any of this because I want you to feel bad for us. I'm telling you because that kind of tragedy never goes away. It's woven into the fabric of the quilt that makes up our family, and I'm sure you haven't heard the story."

Anna shot her a glance and Gayle smiled through her tears.

"How do I know? Because we don't talk about it. Ever. That was something we promised Jack, about a year after it happened. It was a mistake," Gayle admitted with a harsh laugh. "We never should've agreed, and it's a promise we've all broken at one time or another. Privately, one on one, I've talked to both Nikki and Lena about it many times. I know they lean on each other when the anniversary of his death comes upon us. I've talked to my...um, our father about it. As a family, though? With Jack? Never. And we never talk about it with people outside the family. But I guess you're not outside the family anymore, are you?"

Anna didn't know how to respond. She was still reeling from Gayle's story. She'd imagined a dozen ways this discussion might go, but never this.

"Anyway, all this to say... we were grief-stricken and broken and preoccupied when things were at their worst between Nikki and Steve." Gayle held up both hands in helpless surrender. "And we dropped the ball. A few months after River's death, she got pregnant with Beth. She stopped coming around or calling. And we just let her slip away."

Anna shook her head, and this time she did take Gayle's hand. "That wasn't your fault. Steve did that. He orchestrated it all from the start. You can't blame yourselves."

"We can," Gayle insisted. "And we do. Especially Jack. Once we almost lost her, everything changed. He was all over Nikki, making sure she and Beth were safe, second-guessing her every move. He trained in self-defense so he could teach her how to protect herself. I supported it all one hundred percent. We'd just lost River. We couldn't lose Nikki and Beth, too. What we needed was grief counseling and therapy, but we were so lost and adrift."

Gayle pulled away and sat back against the cushioned booth with a weary sigh.

"We made a lot of mistakes. It's easy to see that now. Nikki and Lena are both smart, savvy, and strong. They don't need us telling them what to do anymore, but old habits die hard. So now we're in this mess and I've got to figure out how to clean it up. And I'm starting with you."

Anna regarded her for a long moment. "So are you saying you're going to let Nikki and Lena spend time with me and not punish them for it?"

Gayle nodded. "That too. But I'd also like to get to know you myself. If you're willing..."

"I'm definitely willing, but I'm curious. Why the sudden change of heart?"

Gayle drained the last of her tea and pushed the cup away. "I had a long talk with a great friend. She reminded me that tomorrow isn't promised to anyone, and it made me realize that if today were my last day on this earth, I'd have lived it differently. So I'm starting now."

Anna smiled. "That's pretty admirable."

"I'm not all bad," Gayle said with a low laugh.

"Definitely not. In fact, I think you're pretty nice, considering this all got sprung on you. I don't know how I'd have handled it all in your shoes."

"Well, thank you for that. Maybe you can put a good word in with the brats for me." Anna arched a brow and

Gayle grinned. "What? You think they're the only ones with nicknames?"

Anna outright laughed at that as Leah approached.

"More tea or coffee?" she chirped.

They both declined and she laid the check on the table, which Gayle grabbed before Anna could.

"I know Dad will be really happy to hear we've mended fences. I really want to make his golden years good and less stressful. He doesn't need this infighting any more than the rest of us do." She stood and grabbed her coat. "Thanks for meeting with me, Anna. Do you want to walk out together, or?"

Anna shook her head. "Nah. I've got this soggy pie to eat and all. But thank you for...everything, Gayle."

She watched as Gayle paid the bill at the counter and headed out into the cold, dark night.

If someone had bet her a million dollars that she'd have ended the night with a puddle of tears in front of her and a bittersweet smile on her face, she'd have taken that bet all day. This was not at all what she'd expected, but man, was she glad she'd come.

Her thoughts drifted to Jack...her one and only brother, and the smile faded. Dear God, what that poor man had suffered.

She'd come a long way since she'd gotten to Cherry Blossom Point, but her work wasn't done here yet. It might not be today, or tomorrow, or even on this trip. Someday soon, though, she was going to do her darnedest to fill up her second-family Bingo card.

Buckle up, Jack. Anna Sullivan is coming in for a landing.

18

LENA

Lena shot a glance at the clock and winced. She had to get a move on or she would be late. Another night of unsettling dreams and fitful sleep left her feeling more miserable than ever.

It had been more than twenty-four hours and she still hadn't heard from Owen.

She held off on texting him until she'd put a bagel in the toaster oven and started a cup of coffee, and then she couldn't bear to wait any longer.

Did you get there okay? Lena texted.

Owen's reply came back right away. *Sorry, love. Yeah, here safe.*

Good. Please give everyone my love and let me know if there is anything at all I can do.

She went back to work on breakfast, scrambling some eggs to eat with her bagel, until her phone chimed just as she was plating them up.

I'll be here a couple more days. Just helping them talk through the most awful logistics, a death certificate and funeral arrangements. Gemma's amazing, she's being so strong for the boys. I'm just trying to take some of the worst of it off of her shoulders, and take the boys out so she can get some time to herself. I think they're still in shock, the lot of them. They already paid rent for the first couple months at the house in Mass, so I'm helping them get moved in for now. It will be tough going for a while, but they WILL get through this.

Lena's eyes filled with tears as she thought of Gemma powering through the most devastating loss of her life, being strong for the sake of her sons. For just a moment, she saw Gemma in her mind's eye as a little girl, Owen's mischievous kid sister, and she let out a low groan. She felt so far away and helpless...

I know they will, Lena replied. *They're lucky to have you.*

She made a mental note to call a local restaurant and have food sent to the house. The last thing they needed to be thinking about right now was feeding all those people.

The typing symbol on Owen's end blinked on and off for a few minutes, and Lena set her phone aside. A few minutes later, a message finally came through.

Thank you for being there for me the other night. I'm sorry for drinking so much, and I'm sorry if I did anything stupid. Forgive me. I never want to do anything to lose you.

Lena pushed her plate away and swallowed past the ache in her throat. Just as she'd told Nikki, it had been a stupid mistake after one whiskey too many. He probably didn't even remember...

You never will, she texted back. *See you soon.*

Lena dumped her dishes in the sink and got dressed for work. She needed to pick up three of Freddie's paintings from the framer's this morning and drop them at a gallery a few towns over. When she arrived at the shop and saw the pieces, time stopped for just a moment.

She sometimes forgot why she had put up with Freddie for so long.

This was why.

He had painted these as a set a few years ago, a commission that had fallen through. Lena had pulled them out of storage the month before and found a gallery that wanted them. One showed deer in the woods at dawn, the shadows of the trees falling in lines across the forest floor. Upon a long look, the tree trunks transformed into the bars of a prison cell. The brush in the backdrop revealed itself to be the slumped form of a broken man.

Another painting had ancient, weathered skeletons hidden amongst the leaves on the forest floor. The third showed a woodland meadow in spring; tiny mice clung to long shoots of grass, and the ghost of a girl peered out from the shadows of the trees.

The man could paint. Why did he keep throwing himself into other projects? It was Van Gogh working at mediocre sculptures until his fingers bled, Frida Kahlo at a pottery wheel making lumpy bowls.

All right, so maybe not quite that stark... but senseless, all the same.

Lena loaded the paintings carefully into her car and plugged the gallery address into her phone. Eighty-seven minutes.

Great.

The silence in the car was unbearable, and every radio station grated on her nerves. Her fingers itched to dial Gayle's number and ask her advice, but she hadn't heard from Anna yet about their meeting last night, and she wasn't going there until she did.

Dad.

He could always be counted on to pick up her calls. But this wasn't a phone-call-from-the-freeway conversation. She needed to talk to her dad, and she wanted to see him face to face.

Freddie could wait.

Lena's stomach was beginning to protest the paltry breakfast she had eaten at home, so she stopped by Sadie's cafe on the way to Eric's house. Two breakfast sandwiches to go and a box of macarons for good measure.

"Hey, Lena. Uh, is Jack alright?" Sadie asked as she rang her up. "I saw him at the grocery store last night and he looked terrible."

Lena's stomach turned over in surprise. Apparently her brother was back in town. That was good, at least.

"I don't know," Lena admitted. "We're currently not speaking."

Sadie gave her a sad, knowing look. She knew better than anyone else how Jack shut the world out when he was struggling. It was one of the main reasons that they'd divorced. Jack and River's mom, Corinne, hadn't been together when River passed away. They'd been friends, though, accepting the fact that they weren't good together as a couple but had been blessed with an amazing son. As the years passed and River grew, so did Jack and Corinne. Lena was pretty sure they were on the road to getting back together when tragedy struck and River died in Jack's care. Jack had never forgiven himself for not being able to protect his son.

He had convinced himself that Corinne should never forgive him either.

A year later, Sadie had found him. By that point, Jack had settled into a shaky state of denial, cutting off contact with Corinne, pretending River had never existed most of the time, and nearly drinking himself to death every six months or so.

Sadie had been like a beacon of hope for him...for all of them. Lena had prayed that she would be able to drag him out of the darkness. And for a while, it seemed like she might. They'd gotten married and had a son together, and things seemed good between them. But the older Jack's second son had gotten, the more Jack's grief and fear had come to the surface. He had been simultaneously cold and overprotective, neither openly affectionate in the way that he had been with his first son nor adventurous and fun-loving, despite Sadie's pleas that he just let Wyatt be a kid.

In the end, through no fault of sweet Sadie's, he had lost his wife *and* his living son. By the time Wyatt was fourteen, he stopped seeing Jack altogether. He was seventeen now. He went to a special boarding school in Switzerland that allowed him to explore his passion for skiing, and he wanted nothing to do with his father.

Lena pushed aside the maudlin thoughts and made a mental note to send her nephew a text. It had been a couple months since she'd talked to him, and she missed him dearly.

"It's probably not my place to say anymore," Sadie began, and Lena interrupted her.

"You're family, Sadie. Always."

Her former sister-in-law gave her a sweet, sorrowful smile and continued, "You have to take the bull by the horns and force yourself back in. *Make* him talk to you. The longer you let him stew, the deeper he goes into himself, and the harder it is to bring him back out."

Lena knew she was right. She also knew she couldn't let herself repeat her family's mistakes. She wouldn't let fear run her life. The results were sometimes almost as tragic as the thing that caused the fear in the first place.

"Thank you, Sadie."

"Anytime, sister."

Lena drove to Eric's house, and his face lit up when he opened the door.

"What a wonderful surprise! To what do I owe this weekday visit?"

"I missed you," she said simply. "And I wanted to talk."

"Come in, come in." Eric wrapped her in a firm hug and then stepped back. "Do I smell Sadie's breakfast sandwiches?"

"You've got a good nose," Lena laughed.

"It helps that her name is on the bag. Come on through, I'll pour us some orange juice and Pelligrino."

Lena set out the sandwiches in the sunroom, and Eric joined her with their drinks.

"Did you hear that Gayle called Anna?" she asked

"Nikki told me. They met last night, yes?"

"They were supposed to. I haven't heard from them, but it means a lot that Gayle reached out."

At least, Lena hoped that's what Gayle was doing. The odds were three to one that she was trying to make peace... with the *one* being a sleep-with-the-fishes style chat where she warned Anna to get out of town and never show her face in Cherry Blossom Point again.

"Look there," Eric said suddenly. Lena followed his gaze and saw a cardinal perched on the feeder outside.

"Mom's favorite bird," she remembered.

"I like to think she's keeping an eye on us, sending the cardinals from heaven to look in on us, get a bird's eye view." Eric winced. "It sounds ridiculous when I say it out loud."

"I don't think it's ridiculous," Lena said softly. "I can always feel her when I see cardinals, too."

"Maybe I'm fooling myself with this, but I truly believe that your mom would be happy that Anna finally found her way here. She couldn't face it in life, but maybe now... she would like Anna. Anna the person, you know, not just the idea of her, the memory of my betrayal. She would be happy to see you and Nikki happy, that's the main thing."

"And you."

"And me," he agreed quietly. "Anna brings something good to our lives."

"She does. And to hell with what anyone in town thinks about it."

"To hell with them." Eric smiled at her, and then his expression turned thoughtful. "What else? What's going on with you, chickadee?"

Lena smiled. How long since he had called her by the childhood nickname that only he had used? Then she thought of Owen, and her smile faded.

"Gemma's husband died a few days ago."

"Oh, that poor family," Eric said. "Doesn't she have two young boys?"

Lena nodded. "Owen went to help... my heart is just breaking for her."

Eric nodded sympathetically and took her hand. They

were silent for a time, and finally Lena broached the subject that had brought her here.

"I think I'm having a midlife crisis."

Her father chuckled. "Oh? I didn't see a Ferrari out front."

"I mean it, Dad."

Eric squeezed her hand. "I'm listening."

"Freddie pays me well, but I want to do something more fulfilling."

"That doesn't sound like a midlife crisis. That sounds like a career change that's long overdue."

"I have an idea," she admitted hesitantly. "It's just a germ of one right now, but I'd love to know what you think."

Eric smiled, giving her his complete attention. That had always been his most wonderful character trait. He had worked long hours all through her childhood, but when he was home, he was *home*. He was so present, so focused on his children in the most loving, supportive way.

"I want to create a website. Kind of like eBay," she teased gently, as Nikki had told her about their dad's recent acquisitions, "but for local artists. All kinds of art. Owen's glass, Anna's photographs, those gorgeous scarves and shawls that Bertha knits. And other things, too. Jo's syrups, Sophie's macarons, the Stevensons' goat milk soaps, even Mrs. Keen's jams and jellies and maple syrup candies. I thought I might call it *A Touch of Maine*."

"Lena, that's brilliant."

"Really? You think so?"

"It sounds absolutely perfect for you. You have such an eye for art, and such a wonderful way with people. You're so organized and smart. Take the leap, Lena. You'll soar. I know you will."

"I'm scared, Dad."

"That's when you need to be at your most brave. I still regret not following my dreams. The things in my life that I let fear steal from me... I don't want to see you carry the same regrets. Anything that I can do to help, I'm in. Can I help you with the books, maybe? I'm still aces with numbers, and retirement is terribly dull sometimes."

"I would love that." Working with her dad would be a joy, and it would help him stay sharp. Lena planned to keep her father around as long as humanly possible. One hundred and two seemed reasonable. "It's going to be a while before I get it all together. I haven't told Freddie yet. I think I might just keep working for him while I put it all together..."

"Just don't wait too long, sweetie. Dreams are slippery things, and they can get away from us before we know it."

They cleared the table together, and Lena gave her dad a long hug before she left, feeling positive as she headed out to her car.

It might not happen overnight, but she could do it. She could create something of her own and showcase all of the amazing artists and artisans that she had come to know over the years. Then she would be able to stomp the embers of her stupid, persistent crush on Owen and find happiness in other areas of her life.

She couldn't lose him as a friend.

She was just about to pull out of her father's driveway when her phone buzzed. It was a group text from Gayle to her and Nikki.

Snacks and chat at my house tonight, seven o'clock?

Three little dots were still rolling and a second message followed shortly after.

Anna too...

Lena blinked and read it again, but the message didn't disappear or change.

Things must've gone well between them last night. Part of her wanted to call and get all the details, but the bigger, smarter part wasn't about to look a gift horse in the mouth.

She shot back a quick *yes* and grinned as Nikki's response popped up on the screen a second later.

Yes for both me and Anna.

"Well, I'll be..."

19

GAYLE

Gayle

It was almost time for her guests to arrive as she stood at her kitchen counter, rolling cream cheese and green chilis into tortillas and cutting them into slices. The concoction was an old family recipe that brought back memories of her mother and grandmother, and she knew Lena and Nikki would appreciate them.

Anna might think they were weird, but that was alright. Gayle had decided right out the gate that, if she was going to embrace this whole thing – or accept it, at least – she was going to do it right. That meant no secrets, no hiding the crazy in a closet somewhere only to have it resurface ten years from now.

Anna would see what Anna was going to get, and it wasn't always pretty or fun — and yeah, sometimes it was weird.

She heard the faint sound of the television from the living room — Rex binge-watching another one of his true crime shows. She did not understand the appeal. Why did people watch such miserable things? Wasn't the whole point of entertainment to *escape*?

The doorbell rang, and her mouth went dry. Unlike at the diner, there was no option to flee if she felt overwhelmed. It was sink or swim.

No matter, Gayle thought as she walked through the house, past the place where Rex sat sprawled on the couch. She would put on a brave face for her siblings. After all, she had plenty of practice. In fact, she realized with a start, neither Lena nor Nikki had ever seen her cry, except when River and Mom passed away.

"Hey," Lena said as she opened the door. "I brought wine. Am I the first one here?"

"Sure are." Gayle greeted her sister with a tentative hug, which Lena returned full-force. "Come help me in the kitchen."

"Hi, Rex," Lena said as they walked through the living room.

He let out a muffled sound that might have been, "Hey, Lena."

"Thank you for having us all over tonight," Lena said, emphasis on the *all.* "It means a lot. I know it was only a few days, but not talking to you was awful. For me, at least. Let's not do that again, okay?"

Gayle's heart twisted as she stowed Lena's coat and then set to work slicing manchego for the cheese board. Sometimes she wondered if her sisters saw her as some sort of robot. And it was no wonder. She didn't show them her sadness over living so far from her children, hardly even acknowledged to herself the rage and betrayal that she felt at Rex's affair...

"You need to let them in more," Jo had told her that

afternoon at the pub as Gayle was prepping to leave. *"They're not little girls anymore, Gayle. Lena's, what, forty-six? And Nikki's kid is in college. They're grown-ass women, just like you. Don't use the big sister card as an excuse to keep them at arm's length. It's just a bad habit at this point, kid."*

She'd agreed to try, but it would be a process. She wasn't even sure she knew how to *not* put on a façade with them, it had been so ingrained...

"You made Mom's pinwheels!" Lena said happily, downing a slice in one bite. She swallowed and asked, "I know he wasn't on the text but is Jack coming?"

"No." Gayle shook her head and looked down, slicing salami. "He's not...quite there yet."

Lena's shoulders drooped a little. "Have you even heard from him?"

"Yeah, he texted me."

It was just two words. *I'm fine*. But still, he'd replied.

"I'll deal with Jack another day," Gayle said, looking up at her golden-haired sister. "How are *you*?"

"I'm—" Lena began, and the doorbell rang again. They both went to answer it.

"Hey!" Nikki said with a grin. "Watch out, I brought cake." She pushed past them and went straight for the kitchen.

Gayle's eyes met Anna's, and her voice caught in her throat for a second. She'd replayed their talk over in her mind a hundred times and was still surprised that she'd managed to spill her guts like that to a near stranger. It hadn't been nearly as hard as the idea of fully opening up to Nikki and Lena.

Still, seeing her now definitely felt awkward.

Get used to it and then it will be less awkward, a little voice in her head chirped.

"Hey, Anna," Lena said with a wide smile. "Come on in."

"Welcome," Gayle managed. Anna crossed the threshold, and Gayle gestured vaguely towards her husband. "That's Rex. Rex, this is Anna."

"Hi," Rex said with a clipped nod as he turned off the TV with a sigh. "I know how loud you ladies get, so I'm going to duck out for a couple hours. Save me some of that cake."

He went out through the garage door and Gayle led Anna and Lena into the kitchen, cheeks burning with anger and shame. She knew exactly where he was going, and her sisters probably did too. She could feel Lena's eyes boring a hole in her back.

"Who wants an apple martini? None of that neon green stuff," Gayle said with a tight smile. "The real deal. Homemade green apple schnapps."

"Sounds great," Anna said. "Homemade schnapps, huh? I've had it, but how do you make it?"

"Just alcohol, fruit, and sugar. In this case, apples and vodka. I used some star anise, too."

"I'm in."

Gayle hung Anna and Nikki's coats on the back of a chair with Lena's and then set to work, letting out a breath as she fell into the rhythm of the familiar task of making drinks.

Getting comfortable with Anna was going to take some time. Still, she didn't feel nauseous when she looked at her this time.

She'd log that as a win.

"Have a pinwheel," Lena said to Anna, gesturing to the neat little snacks.

"Wow, that's oddly delicious," Anna said after a moment.

"We used to make them every holiday growing up. It was our thing. And it was something we could make ourselves, even when we were really little. We always felt so grown up, making our own contribution to the celebration."

"Which reminds me," Anna said, and Gayle glanced over her shoulder to see Anna pull a bottle of wine from her massive purse. Lena laughed in delight.

"I brought the same one!"

"Oh. Sorry."

"No, it's a good thing! It's Gayle's favorite."

Her sisters were nervous, Gayle reflected. Lena was over-bright and Nikki had been silent, putting the finishing touches on the cheese board that Gayle had started. Hopefully martinis would take the edge off for them all. She handed them out, taking a pull from her glass.

Icy cold, tart perfection, if she did say so herself.

Anna's eyebrows shot up when she tasted hers.

"This is delicious!"

"There's a reason she owns a bar," Nikki said.

"The woman's an artist," Lena added.

Gayle thanked them with a smile, oddly touched by the praise. She was still feeling a little bruised from their fight, and a reminder that they were proud of her in spite of all her faults helped. She'd feared that it had gone so far for so long that they'd stop seeing Gayle at all and just pictured her as the Wicked Witch of the West riding in on a broom...

"That's like my sister Cee-cee and cupcakes," Anna said. "They're phenomenal."

"They really are," Nikki agreed.

"Sometimes people are just born with a knack."

"Let's sit down," Gayle said, carrying the cheese board over to the dining table. "I don't know how Lena even walks in those heels. Your feet must be killing you, sis."

"I'm used to them," Lena said, but she kicked her shoes off as she spoke.

"I hear congratulations are in order?" Gayle said, turning her attention to Nikki.

Nikki beamed, some of the tension leaving her face. "Did Lena tell you?"

"I heard it through the grapevine."

"If you ever open a wine bar, you should call it that!" Lena laughed.

"The job hasn't started yet," Nikki continued, "but it's an absolute dream. I'm so excited. The restaurant is brand new, so not exactly job security... but I think it will make it. Either way, it'll be one helluva ride."

Gayle raised her glass. "To one helluva ride!"

They all cheersed to Nikki, and silence settled over the table as they tasted the food that Gayle had set out.

"I picked these up at the bookstore," Nikki said as she reached into her bag and pulled out a deck of cards. Gayle held out her hand so she could read the back of the box.

TABLETOPIX: Conversation Starters

"Oh, God, noooo," Gayle groaned with a chuckle.

"Don't knock it 'til you try it!" Nikki shot back, taking the cards back from her. "I thought it would be fun to have some ice breakers. Get to know Anna a bit better, let her get to know you guys... I bet you'll even learn something about Lena and me that you don't know. It has four levels, basic questions down to deeper ones."

"And we'll pry some secrets out of you," Lena said playfully, waggling her brows as Gayle. "I'm in."

"Fine," Gayle said, shoving back the sudden rush of fear.

Let the opening up commence.

"Anna?" Nikki offered her the box. "Will you do the honors?"

Anna accepted the box with the expression Gayle might expect from someone handling a live snake. Her expression relaxed when she read the first card.

"Favorite movie. Easy. *Fiddler on the Roof.* Nikki?"

"You know that's my favorite movie too," Nikki laughed. "Lena?"

Lena thought for a moment. "*Some Kind of Wonderful.* Gayle? What's your favorite?"

"I don't really watch movies much," she replied honestly. Who had the time? Besides, Rex always had control of the remote. Then, a memory came to her, and she smiled. "Actually, I guess it's *The Sound of Music*. It was my favorite growing up, and I watched it on repeat with my kids, too."

"That's another favorite of mine," Anna said. "Anything with Julie Andrews. Have you seen *Victor Victoria*?"

"I don't think I have."

"Maybe next time we get together, we do a movie night."

Next time we get together.

She had been so focused on getting through tonight, she hadn't thought much about next time...

She swallowed hard. "Sounds good."

"No movies tonight!" Nikki said, holding up a hand. "Only secrets!" She had finished her martini, Gayle noticed, and had just poured a glass of the wine that Lena had brought. Their baby sister didn't drink much, and it showed. She pulled a card from the bottom of the deck.

"If you could ask anyone for help, who would it be and why?" Nikki was suddenly teary-eyed. "Aw...it would be you guys."

"I go to my big sisters," Anna said with a nod. "Every time."

"Yeah, it's you guys for me, too, and then Dad," Lena said.

"Aaaand?" Nikki urged.

"Um, I guess Owen." Lena's cheeks turned pink. "Gayle? How about you?"

"I'd have to go with Jack. Actually, Jo first...then Jack."

How sad was it that her husband didn't make the cut, and wouldn't, even if she had to list her top ten?

"Oh man," Nikki said. "Me too. Redo. I choose Jo. We aren't close like her and Gayle, but Jo gets the job *done*."

"She does seem like a force of nature," Anna said approvingly. "I'm going with Jo, too," Anna said, causing the rest of them to burst out laughing.

They all turned to Gayle expectantly, so she reached into the box and gingerly removed a card.

She scanned it quickly and let out a relieved sigh. "Okay, so what's the weirdest thing you've ever eaten?" Gayle wrinkled her nose. "I think it has to be rocky mountain oysters. When we stayed with Rex's brother at his ranch. They didn't tell me what they were until *after* I'd eaten them. Rex thought it was hilarious."

"What are rocky mountain oysters?" Lena asked.

"You don't want to know," Gayle said with a wince.

"Let's just say that they come from a bull, and leave it at that. What about you, Nikki?"

Nikki thought for a moment. "Pork brains and eggs."

"No!" Lena shouted as Anna laughed.

"Yep. In Arkansas. With grits." She shrugged. "It was good."

"This calls for another round," Gayle said. She stood and went to pour them each some of her sapphire-colored vodka in glasses of sparkling water with ice.

"Lena?" Nikki asked behind her.

"Probably that spaghetti pizza you used to make in high school," Lena deadpanned.

"What about those s'more burgers she made with the chocolate and marshmallows?" Gayle asked, faking a gag as she joined them back at the table.

"Oh yuck, you're right. Those were way weirder."

"Weirder than my green chili sundae?" Nikki asked.

"That was weirdly delicious," Lena laughed. "I think that was when you started to actually get a hang of the whole cooking thing. And hey, if eating that stuff helped get you to where you are now, I'll be your guinea pig any day. "What about you, Anna?"

"Oh man. Too many to pick just one. I traveled for a living, remember?"

"Top five!" Nikki urged.

"*Chapulines* in Mexico. That's fried grasshoppers. Would not recommend. Durian fruit in Thailand. Some people say it smells awful, but I loved it. It tastes *amazing*. Haggis in Scotland," she continued, ticking off fingers as she went. "That was pretty good, but I hadn't eaten in, like, two days. What else?

Fugu in Japan, that's pufferfish. I tried some grubs in Australia that were pretty good, if I didn't actually look at what I was eating. That's five, right? I've eaten a *lot* of bugs, you guys. Way too many bugs." Anna covered her face. "Next question, please!"

Lena pulled a card and read, "What is your earliest memory?" She smiled. "I think it's that beach in Rhode Island. We went when I was four, I think? I remember running barefoot, and the sand was so hot. Dad scooped me up and put me on his shoulders, then ran straight for the water. The waves were washing over his head, but he never let me go under."

Gayle remembered that day too, because all the running around and pollen in the air had triggered an asthma attack. They'd spent the evening in the E.R. and once they'd gotten back to their hotel, she'd slept on the floor next to Lena's bed because she'd been so scared her sister might stop breathing.

"I loved that beach," Gayle said, clearing her suddenly too-tight throat. "We went a few times. Mom's cousin lived nearby. It was so lovely there."

"What's your earliest memory?" Lena asked.

Gayle smiled fondly at her sister. "Actually, it's you. I remember watching you move inside of mom's belly. Jack would run out of the room every time she showed us. He was terrified that you were going to burst out through her skin, like some sort of alien. But I thought it was the most amazing thing. And I remember the day she brought you home. Your head was covered in white-blonde fuzz. Lord, you were cute."

"Well, *my* first memory is *you*," Nikki said with a hiccup.

Gayle surreptitiously pushed the plate of bread and brie closer to her sister and made a mental note to slow down the drink service.

"I remember lying on my belly on the floor," Nikki told her, "trying to see out under the door. It was past my bedtime, and Mom and Dad had friends over for dinner. You came and scooped me up and put me back in bed. You must have been... twelve?"

"You always mothered us," Lena said to Gayle. Then, she looked over to Anna. "What about you?"

Anna's expression was shuttered and she took a long drink before replying. "Pop...my dad. I remember holding his hand, but my hand was so tiny that I just wrapped it around his thumb. Walking through town with him, feeling so safe and special. He was a good egg. A pain in the butt sometimes, but a really good egg."

Gayle could feel the grief rolling off her, and her own heart gave a squeeze. "You must miss him a lot."

"I do. I really do." Anna sucked in a breath and forced a smile as she reached for the deck. "Alrighty, let's see what we have here," she murmured, pulling another card. "Weird. This one has Lena's name on it, and it says 'How come you haven't scooped up that sexy Irishman yet?'"

Gayle laughed in surprise and Nikki straight-up cackled, but Lena was not amused.

"What does it actually say?" she said with a scowl.

"I swear." Anna looked at her with wide, innocent eyes. "That's what it says. You have to answer. Them's the rules."

"Yeah, well, no one said anything about bathroom breaks, and I'm taking one," Lena shot back, cheeks flaming as she scurried out of the room.

"Too far?" Anna asked with a grimace.

"Not in my book. Someone's gotta say it," Nikki said.

"Eat some bread, Nik," Gayle told her.

"Try it with the brie," Anna chimed in.

Nikki took a bite and then shot up from the table. "Actually, I gotta pee too."

"Lena's—"

"I'll use your bathroom."

"Don't worry," Anna said as Nikki disappeared. "I can drive us. Do you think Lena's okay? I really didn't mean to upset her."

"She'll be fine. I've wanted to ask her the same thing for ages, but, well... love isn't exactly my area of expertise."

"Haven't you been married for decades?"

Gayle had nearly forgotten who she was talking to. Anna, the only person who *wasn't* up-to-date on town gossip. But Anna must have seen something in Gayle's eyes, because her expression changed and she nodded, despite Gayle not saying a word.

"Gotcha," she said quietly. "I'm sorry to hear that."

Nikki came back in and hugged Gayle from behind her chair.

"Thank you."

"For what?" Gayle asked.

"Just for trying. You know? Thanks for trying. I know you mostly did it for me and Lena, and I love you for it."

She sat back down and stuffed a chili pinwheel in her mouth. Gayle couldn't help but smile. Drunk Nikki reminded her a lot of little-kid Nikki.

Lena came back to the table a short while later, and Anna let her off the hook. Over the next two hours, they worked their way through the entire deck of cards—and the cake that Nikki had made.

No one saved a slice for Rex.

Anna and Nikki were the first to go. Anna thanked Gayle for her hospitality and hauled Nikki home to sleep it off.

"I should get going, too," Lena said a few minutes after they drove away. Gayle didn't argue as she donned her coat, picked up her purse, and hugged Gayle goodbye.

"Hey, Lena?" Gayle said, unable to hold her tongue a second longer.

"Yeah?"

"I'm not trying to boss you or mother you, or any of that. But I need you to know something." She brushed a wild, golden curl from her younger sister's eye and held her gaze intently. "You deserve love. You deserve Owen, or at least someone who treats you like he does. You put up with second-rate guys for too long, and then you let Frederick walk all over you. You deserve better."

Lena looked at her for a long time and then nodded. "So do you, Gayle." With one last hug, she turned and left without another word.

Gayle stood rooted to her spot for a long while...long enough for Lena's car to pull out of the driveway, and Rex's to take its place.

He walked in the house a few minutes later and stopped short when he found her standing, motionless in the hallway.

"What are you doing?" he muttered as he made to shoulder past her, reeking of cheap perfume.

And suddenly, it was all so clear.

She grabbed his arm and tugged him to a stop.

"We need to talk."

20

LENA

LENA STOOD at her bathroom mirror, applying a subtle-but-visible amount of makeup. The last thing she needed was Freddie commenting on how tired she looked. She'd had a great night with her sisters, but she still slept like garbage. Between Anna's question and Gayle's parting words, she'd been up most of the night tossing and turning. At this rate, she should buy stock in concealer, because she was going through it by the bucketload.

Her phone buzzed and she picked it up, expecting a breakfast order from Freddie. Her brain registered Owen's name just as she touched the green circle to accept the call.

"Good morning, love." He sounded weary and her heart gave a squeeze.

"Hey, there," she murmured, wishing she could give him a big hug, and hating that, even if he was close enough to receive it, she would've hesitated.

God, why had she let things get so weird between them?

"Thank you for the food you sent for Gemma and the kids. So appreciated."

"Of course," she replied, setting the bathroom counter back in order just to have something to do with her hands. "It's the least I can do. How's it going down there?"

"It's going," he replied with a sigh. "I don't think there is much else I can do for right now. I'm just taking up a guest room, and Jerry's brother and sister got into town last night. I'm going to head back home this afternoon."

"Is Gemma coming with you?"

"Not right now. She and her in-laws are still working out the details of the memorial service before they head back home. They're going to hold it in upstate New York, where he grew up, so I'll head there for that. He'll be cremated, so they're going to wait until after Christmas in hopes it will be less traumatic for the kids. I offered to stay longer, but I think Gemma wants to get the planning done and then be alone for a bit to process. She's still somewhat in shock, I think. I asked if she wanted me to take the boys off her hands at some point, but for now they just want to be together and grieve. I told her I could drive back down at the drop of a hat."

"You're a good brother, Owen." *And a good man,* she reflected. She was so lucky to have him in her life.

Which was exactly why she couldn't risk ruining that, no matter what her sisters tried to say.

"I should be home by dinnertime if you want to meet for a burger," he continued. "I could use the company and a chance to decompress. We can go to Rusty's Place, if you want."

His heart must be breaking for his poor sister and her family right now, so anything she could do to take even a little of that edge off, she was more than willing.

"That's okay, we can go to The Milky Thistle."

There was a long pause. "Wait, does that mean you and your sister are speaking again, then?"

"Yep. Get this...She's even speaking to Nikki and Anna."

He let out a low whistle. "Will wonders never cease?"

Owen was trying to keep it light, so she followed suit. "It's a banner day. The Milky Thistle is back in play."

"Lord be praised. I'd do it for you, but it would've been hard to give up those burgers. I look forward to you distracting me with the whole story."

"Glad to be of service. What's your ETA?"

"I'm thinking around 8, but I'll call you when I'm close." Owen paused, and for a moment, Lena wondered if the call had dropped. Then, he said, "I've missed you, love."

Lena swallowed hard and forced a reply past the lump in her throat. "See you tonight."

"Lena," Owen said, his tone unusually thick and serious.

"I've gotta get to work," she cut him off reflexively as a bolt of panic shot through her. "Drive safe." She hung up and stuffed her phone in her purse.

Geez, what was *wrong* with her? Maybe a therapist could help her get past all of these unbearable feelings.

But, for now, she had to focus on the matter at hand.

Freddie.

Between the talk with her dad, being around her sisters last night, and all her middle-of-the-night ruminating, she'd made a decision. She wasn't going to let those slippery dreams get away. She was going for it, and she was going for it *today*.

You can do this...

Freddie greeted her at the door fifteen minutes later, which was unusual.

"You're finally here!"

And five minutes early to boot, she thought, but bit back the swift retort as he took her by the arm and all but dragged her inside.

"Come on. My matchstick sculpture is complete. You've got to see it!"

It wasn't even nine in the morning and Lena could smell the absinthe. This couldn't be good...

She walked in and Freddie spread his arms, making a grand gesture towards his matchstick monstrosity. It was impressive... for a fifth-grade art project. She could see what he'd been trying to do. It was an Escher-esque cityscape, somewhere between a dreamscape and a nightmare. She could *see* what it would look like if it were pigment on canvas, one of his brilliant paintings. As it was, the thing was uneven and unimpressive, a confusing mess of wood and visible clumps of glue. She had to squint and move from side to side to even differentiate one feature from another.

"So?" Freddie asked as he shifted from foot to foot, gaze drilling into her. "What do you think?"

What did she think?

She *thought* it was *Rubber Duckies* all over again. She had tried to be supportive back then, bolstering his delicate ego, trying to give him the encouragement he so clearly wanted. There hadn't been much of a choice; he had created the thing *in* the art museum, hanging each duckie from the ceiling with fishing line over a massive porcelain bathtub that had been cracked in two. They had worked right up until opening night, and at that point, there was nothing to do but run with it. But this...

"It's crap, Frederick."

His jaw swung wide and he started blinking so fast that for a second she wondered if he was having a stroke.

She shrugged. "I'm sorry if that's not what you want to hear, but it's the truth. You know it. I know it. Let's skip the weeks of trying to pretend this works and just cut to the chase. It's a fail, and that's *okay*. It's part of your process. Put it in the attic with the rest of them, and let's move along to the next masterpiece, shall we?"

He raked a hand through his bleached hair and finally found his voice.

"Why are you trying to hurt me this way? It's like...I don't even know who you are right now," he said brokenly.

"Lena two-point-oh." Lena took Freddie by his slender shoulders and steered him towards the stairs. "Come on."

"What are you doing?" he protested.

"Walk," she commanded, and he climbed the staircase. When they reached the top, she pointed to the painting that hung there. "Look at that."

He gave it a cursory glance, and Lena said, "No. Look. When's the last time you really looked at it?"

Frederick turned to regard the canvas, and his face softened slightly.

"It's good," he said finally, with a grudging nod.

"It's not good. It's amazing. Transcendent. You're a frigging genius, Frederick. *This* is your medium. Not matchsticks. Not rubber ducks. Not plastic teeth," she said, wincing as she recalled one particularly horrific experiment that they had both made a tacit agreement never to mention again.

Frederick laughed shakily, still looking at the painting.

"Stay right there," Lena told him.

"Someone's feeling froggy today," he murmured under his breath. He sounded almost...grateful?

Maybe there was something to this bossy thing, after all.

She had stocked the fridge the day before, so there was food in the kitchen for once. After sliding two bagels in the toaster oven, she cut up some red onions.

"Maybe it's time to just accept it. Paint is your medium, and you don't have the ability to just crank them out," Lena told Frederick as she prepared them a meal of smoked salmon and cream cheese. "Instead of burning your energy on bizarre experiments, you need to take some time to recharge between paintings. Go outside, travel, seek inspiration instead of trying to manufacture it."

"Ugh," he groaned, tearing himself away from the painting and sitting on a barstool to face her. "I hate it when you're right."

"Well, hate it in silence while you eat," Lena said, putting a plate in front of him.

She joined him and took a bite of her bagel with lox. Salty and creamy and rich and crunchy. Such decadent comfort food. They finished their food in silence, listening to the classical music that Freddie had on downstairs. Then, Lena put their plates in the dishwasher, and Freddie wandered back down to the first floor. Lena followed to find him staring at his matchstick sculpture. He circled it, staring in quiet contemplation.

Then, suddenly, he began to laugh. And he kept laughing, working himself into full on hysterics. Finally he got control of himself and turned to Lena with a wry smile.

"Oh my God. Seriously, though. Look at that mess. How do you put up with me?"

"Damned if I know." Lena smiled back at him.

Frederick went rummaging through boxes and came back with a miniature sledgehammer and a baseball bat. He offered the latter to Lena.

"Shall we?"

She took the bat, and Frederick swung at one of the sculpture's misshapen towers. It flew off of the table and landed on the floor, where Freddie proceeded to stomp it to bits. He looked at Lena expectantly, and she took a swing at the sculpture. Instead of breaking, the whole thing went flying off of the metal table and skidded across the concrete floor. Frederick chased after it and gleefully jumped up and down until the entire project was nothing but splinters on the floor.

"Feel better?" Lena asked.

"It was very cathartic." Frederick flopped onto the couch. He looked at her with one raised eyebrow. "You know you're going to have to clean that up, right?"

Lena laughed and joined him on the couch, where he shot her a confused look.

"So riddle me this, Lena 2.0. How will I maintain the luxurious lifestyle to which I've become accustomed?" he asked by sweeping a hand around him.

This was it. This was her opening.

"You can start by learning how to do some things for yourself... and hiring a much less expensive assistant."

Freddie blanched. "Ew, why?"

She stared at him for a long moment and his face, pink from his exertions, suddenly went pale as the color drained away. "Lena, shut up. Don't even say it."

"It's time for me to make a change," she said, willing herself to say the words before she chickened out. "I've thought about my strengths and my passion and what I want to do with my life, and I realized that it isn't this. I love you—even though you drive me crazy—but it's always been about the art for me. I love sniffing out something special and amazing to share with other people. I've got enough savings, and I've decided to go for it. I'm going to start a new website where I can represent dozens of local artists and craftspeople, maybe hundreds. No more coffee runs. No more grocery shopping or trips to the hardware store. Just *art*, in all its forms." She let out a shuddery breath, feeling a hundred pounds lighter and almost effervescent with hope and excitement. "I think I can do it."

Freddie opened and closed his mouth several times, looking for all the world like a fish out of water. Lena could tell that he wanted to beg her to stay, like he had so many times before. But when he finally spoke, it was like a switch had flipped inside him.

"I know you can do it. Good luck, Lena. You deserve it." He sounded so composed and mature, it nearly brought a tear to her eye. "I... I would love it if you'd consider representing me."

"Seriously?" she asked, her eyes nearly bugging out of her head. "You realize you'd have to," she flipped up a pair of finger quotes, "sell out, right? I mean, this is a commercial website. You might even have to sell," she lowered her voice to a scandalous whisper, "prints."

Frederick's expression suggested that someone was shoving a dagger beneath his fingernail... but after a moment, he nodded.

"Yeah, yeah, I get it. And I'd do it if you were at the helm."

Lena grinned, overwhelmed. "You're officially my first client."

He held open his arms and she leaned in for a hug.

This had gone way easier than she'd ever hoped.

"I don't suppose you know any local perfumers that you'll be including in this venture?" Freddie muttered into her hair. "What is that scent, Eau du baby powder? I hate to tell you, but you need to up your game a little." He drew back and shook his head disapprovingly. "That's way more Maryanne when you need to be channeling Ginger."

She leaned back and snorted. "You do know how to ruin a moment, my friend. Need I remind you that I don't have any game to step up?"

If only she'd known that was what had been holding Owen back all this time. She just needed a better perfume.

"Now I'll start getting things in order and updating the assistant's manual I created over the next couple days. Then, on Monday, I'll help you hire a new assistant."

"So soon?" he asked dramatically.

"I'm putting a listing up today," she told him. "By early next week, I'll have a stack of art-school grads for us to interview."

"The horror," Frederick moaned.

"It's going to be great."

She shot a glance at her watch. She had better get to work if she wanted to get a lot done and still have time to go home and change before dinner with Owen. Today was a day for new beginnings and she couldn't wait to clear the air. She could only hope her talk with him would go as well as this one had. That kiss had rocked her to the core and made her question everything. She couldn't go through that again. It was just too hard, and it wasn't fair to her.

Hopefully he would understand and think twice before making another drunken mistake.

Hopefully they could find their way back to the way things were and she could forget how his lips felt on hers, how his arms felt around her hips...

Hopefully.

21

LENA

"Hey, Lena," Jo greeted her as she walked into The Milky Thistle. "Owen's in the corner booth, purple side."

"Thanks, Jo." Lena followed the painted ribbons and LED lights of the aurora borealis to the back corner, where Owen sat waiting. He greeted her with a wan smile and held up the special's menu.

"Bacon and jalapeño jam cheeseburger," he announced with a shadow of his usual cheer. "I know what I'm getting."

"That does sound good," Lena acknowledged as she slid into the booth, trying not to stare at his painfully beautiful face. It was so good to have him back and see for herself that he might be battered and bruised, but he was going to be alright. "I've been craving their chowder, though."

"I'm shocked," Owen joked weakly. The fish chowder was her favorite.

"Hey, Owen." Gayle appeared and gave Lena a one-armed hug. "I was so sorry to hear about your brother-in-law. Those poor boys."

Owen nodded, his stubbled jaw clenched tight. "Thanks, Gayle."

"Give my sympathies to Gemma, would you?"

Lena realized with a start that her sister looked almost as exhausted as she and Owen did. Was she regretting the whole Anna thing already? Lena hoped not. Their girls' night had started off a little awkward, but Anna and Gayle seemed to actually enjoy each other's company after the first round of drinks. It all seemed to be going so well...

But Gayle was definitely looking worse for wear.

"Of course," Owen said, offering Gayle a nod.

"What can I get for you?" she asked.

"The new burger and a pint of the darkest beer you've got."

"You've got it. Lena?"

"I'll have the cod chowder," Lena told her sister.

"And to drink?" Gayle asked.

"Surprise me."

Gayle squeezed her shoulder and moved on to the next table.

"How are you holding up?" Lena asked Owen. "You look tired."

He shrugged. "I'm doing as well as can be expected, love. I'm heartbroken for Gemma and her boys, but there's nothing doing about that."

"And how's *she* holding up?"

"Entirely too well."

"How do you mean?"

"That sounded terrible, didn't it?" Owen gave her a wry smile and patted her hand before slumping back in his seat. "I mean that she hasn't slowed down. She told me to leave so she would have space to grieve, but the woman won't stop moving. She made all of the funeral arrangements while Jerry's folks sat and watched old sitcoms with the boys. She's working on getting a memorial for him at the Boys and Girls Club in Denver where he used to volunteer and starting some kind of scholarship in his name. It's like she's trying to skip the grieving process altogether. She's still in shock and the minute she slows down, it's going to catch up to her. I just hope I'm there when it does."

He was fidgeting, moving the salt and pepper shakers around on the table. Lena reached out to still his hand—but just then, one of the servers came by with their drinks.

"North Sky Stout for you," she said, putting a glass down in front of Owen, "and the Curieux for Lena."

They thanked her and sat sipping their beers for a moment before Owen asked, "And your family? Gayle and Anna? How is the Merrill family drama playing out?"

"They seem to be getting along," Lena said hesitantly.

"Amazing."

"Yeah, well... Jack's still hiding out, so no miracles on that front." She paused. "Did Gayle look tired to you?"

"Not that I noticed."

"She's trying, but I think it's hard on her."

"That woman would go toe to toe with a T-Rex without flinching."

"Probably," Lena laughed.

They chatted for a few minutes about blessedly mundane things until their food arrived.

"Sweet and Spicy Bacon Burger," their server announced, setting down a massive hamburger nestled in a pile of hand-cut fries, "and a bowl of the cod chowder."

"Thanks," Lena acknowledged.

"You're a peach," Owen said with a grin as the waitress laid out his condiments: ketchup, mustard, and even extra jalapeño-bacon jam. As she stepped away, Lena spooned up a huge bite of chowder.

Man, but that was some comfort food. Big morsels of melt-in-your mouth black cod and tiny pieces of bacon in a creamy broth. It was savory and sweet, with fresh herbs and flecks of black pepper. Lena ordered the fish chowder at least once a week all winter long, and it never disappointed.

"You have got to try this burger," Owen said.

Lena looked up from her food to find the burger in her face. She couldn't help but laugh at the absurdity of the man, and some of the tension drained away. She took a bite and made a show of being suitably impressed.

It *was* a good burger. They'd added fresh bacon to Jo's jalapeño jam and spread it liberally over their sharp-cheddar cheeseburger.

"That's delicious," she said after she'd swallowed.

"You've got a bit of jam, just there." Owen reached out to wipe it away, and his thumb lingered on her lip... two seconds two long.

Lena felt an unsettling urge to bite him.

Hard.

What the hell was he about lately?

"Be right back," she announced, and scooted out of the booth like it was on fire. She rushed to the ladies' room and splashed cold water on her face with trembling hands.

Get it together. You were fine around him for years. You'd stuffed all those schoolgirl feelings down nice and deep. What's got you all hot and jumpy?

"He kissed me," she muttered at her reflection.

The memory rushed back in with clear immediacy, and Lena shoved it away.

He was drunk. Now pull yourself together. You're a grown woman, so stop acting like a jittery teenager.

Lena splashed her face again and used a towel to wipe away the mess she'd made of her makeup.

By the time she got back to the table, Owen had devoured his burger and sat eating his fries. As Lena slid back into the booth, he asked, "How's work going? Did Freddie finish his matchstick masterpiece?"

"He did. And then I smashed it with a baseball bat."

Owen paused with a French fry halfway to his mouth, and then laughed so loudly that half of the restaurant turned to look at him.

"You *what*?" he asked once he'd caught his breath. "Tell me everything."

"Well, technically, I knocked it off of the table with a baseball bat and then Frederick sort of... jumped on it. I did have permission," she added with a grin. "I also quit."

"You *what*?" he said again. "Well, it's about time! How'd he take it?"

"Like a gentleman, actually," she said. "I'm going to start my own business. A website that sells local art. I was thinking of calling it *A Taste of Maine.* Once he'd gotten over the initial shock, Frederick was supportive. He asked if he could be a part of it...he even agreed to *prints*."

"Did I make the list?" Owen asked with a soft smile.

"You know perfectly well that you're first on the list if you want to be," she said primly.

"Of course I want to be."

Owen reached out and took her hand in his, sending a hot rush of blood to her cheeks. She hoped that the undulating lavender lighting offered some decent camouflage.

"It's a brilliant idea, love. I am so proud of you." His fingertip began tracing maddening designs on the inside of her wrist and suddenly, something inside her snapped.

"What are you doing, Owen?" she demanded, yanking her hand away. "What is that, even?"

He stared at her in confusion, his mouth slightly open. Lena tore her eyes away from his lips, removing herself from the booth entirely.

"I can't take any more." Her voice was shaking as she fought back the tears that were burning her eyes. "The kiss the other night, the long looks, that *caress*." She lowered her voice to a hiss. "That's not how friends treat each other."

"Lena, I—"

"It's going to be fine," she insisted, brushing away a tear that threatened to fall. "I'm not mad at you, so don't be mad at me, either. Flirting comes as naturally to you as breathing, I get that. But it *means* something to me and it's hurting me, so I need you to stop."

He opened his mouth to speak again but she held up a hand and shook her head as she grabbed her coat.

"Please don't. I'll call you tomorrow, okay?"

She took a stumbling step backwards, then turned and fled. Gayle shot her a look of sympathy as she rushed past and out the door.

The cold air hit her like a bracing slap and she paused on the sidewalk for a deep breath.

She'd meant that to go so differently. In her mind's eye,

she was going to be calm and clear. Just a quick relay of information.

But real life was sloppier than that most of the time, wasn't it?

She just had to hope that once they'd both processed what had just happened, they'd come out the other side of it with their friendship—and her heart—intact.

Because she wasn't sure she could bear it any other way...

22

ANNA

"Almost ready to watch that new zombie movie?" Anna asked Nikki.

They were done with dinner, already showered and changed into their PJs, ready for another movie night. They'd re-watched all of their favorite musicals early in the visit and had since moved on to horror films. Not the kind about human monsters—the Steve incident was too recent for that—but the fun kind, made with prosthetics and fake gore.

"Yeah, the popcorn's just about done." Nikki poured it into a massive metal bowl, then reached into a cabinet and pulled out a mason jar filled with green powder. She proceeded to sprinkle it liberally on the popcorn.

Anna made a face, and Nikki laughed.

"I trust you with food and all, but come on. Popcorn's not supposed to be green."

Nikki just grinned at her and added another shake of her homemade topping. "Garlic scapes, green onions, and summer herbs. Try it."

Anna tried it, and it was phenomenal. Because duh, everything Nikki made was phenomenal.

"I am so sorry for doubting you," Anna said.

"That'll teach you."

"Can you blame me? I've heard tales of s'mores burgers and green chile sundaes." Anna grabbed another handful of popcorn. "Though, I'll admit that I've yet to taste anything of yours that wasn't completely delicious."

"Those were my experimental teen years," Nikki said, tossing a bite of the green popcorn into her mouth. "I've moved on."

"Onwards and upwards!" Anna declared. "Hey, you should put this stuff on the tables instead of bread. At the restaurant. You know how some places have popcorn instead? This is way better than anything else I've tried."

"That's a good idea," Nikki said thoughtfully, "except that we can't get enough local corn to serve popcorn every night. But maybe with the bread... I could use this powder to make an herb butter, and serve it with fresh sourdough."

"That sounds divine."

"Go get the movie ready. I'll make some flavored seltzers. I still have some of the orange-fennel syrup that Jo made."

"Yum." Anna carried the popcorn into the living room and queued up their flick. There was something indescribably cozy about curling up on the couch with her sister, warm and safe from both the chill December wind that blew outside and the horrors of the screen. Anna felt completely at home here, as much as she did at Cee-cee's place or Steph's.

Where would she be right now if she'd said no to meeting Nikki?

The thought still crept up every now and then, and it was a doozy. Right up there with, What if she'd never slowed down long enough to get to know Beckett? Would she still be globe-trotting, far from any of her sisters? Without him and Teddy? Without Beth and Lena? She had lived happily without all of them for half a century, but if she were to lose any one of them now, she would feel bereft.

She would have been content and blissfully unaware had she never met Beckett or the Merrills. But her life would have been the poorer for it. And if she had stuck to her guns when Nikki had come to town and refused to have anything to do with her? There always would have been a niggling sense of unrest, deep down. That constant, haunting What if? The what-ifs haunted her, even now. What if she had been stubborn and stayed away for years, and missed out on ever meeting Eric? Someday, down the line, she would have regretted her choice.

Nikki came in with their drinks and hit Play, and Anna smiled at her. She couldn't wait to introduce Beckett to the whole Merrill clan. Even Gayle seemed to be warming up to her. Anna was hopeful about the future. She was even hopeful about Jack, who hung just outside the circle of family firelight, like a dog that'd been kicked one too many times. She wouldn't scare him off by rushing up to pet him, but if she kept visiting Cherry Blossom Point, slowly moving closer each time, who knew? Maybe he'd sniff her hand by summer.

The movie started, and Anna hunkered deeper into the couch, shoulder to shoulder with Nikki. She was going to miss this. But she missed her Bluebird Bay family, too. Dinners with her sisters, quiet afternoons with Beckett and

Teddy. She'd stay another week or so, and then it was time to head home.

Eric was already planning to visit her in January; Anna wanted to take him on a tour of the preservation society. They always had plenty of rescue birds around. He would love it. Nikki would be in Bluebird Bay plenty to see Mateo, and Anna would convince Lena to ride along when she could; Lena could stay with her and Beckett, if she wanted to. Teddy was sure to charm her.

It was nice to have a big family, and Anna's was bigger than she'd ever imagined.

The movie began to pick up, and Anna's thoughts fell away as she became immersed in another world. The main characters made a narrow escape, taking shelter in an empty house. Zombies surrounded them on every side, and they retreated to a windowless room. There was a moment of silence, and then the door handle began to rattle. There was a loud groan, and—

Nikki's front door burst open. Anna shrieked as Nikki jumped up, sending popcorn flying everywhere. Anna brandished the remote like a weapon, and Nikki held the empty bowl in front of her like a shield as she fumbled for the light switch.

"Geez, what the heck," Lena muttered, holding an arm up against the glare of the lamp as she slammed the door shut behind her. "I'm officially the most awkward human being in the universe," she announced, squinting as her eyes adjusted to the light. "At least, I thought I was until I saw you two. What's going on?"

"Zombie movie," Anna said by way of explanation as her heartbeat slowed from a frantic canter to a trot.

She bent to help Nikki clean up the popcorn while Lena shed her coat, hat, and scarf.

"What happened?" Nikki asked, looking up at Lena.

"Oh, nothing big, I just made a complete fool of myself in front of all the patrons at The Milky Thistle, including Owen, is all."

"Hot cocoa?" Nikki offered as they cleaned up the last of the mess. She headed for the kitchen without waiting for an answer. Her sisters followed and sat on stools at the counter as Nikki busied herself at the stovetop.

"Do you want to give us a little more context on your public humiliation?" Anna asked.

"I just yelled at my best friend in public. Over nothing." Lena set her head down on the counter with a thump, and the rest of her words came out muffled. "The sudden death of his brother-in-law obviously threw him way off balance. He's a mess, and I should be there for him, but *I've* been a mess since he kissed me, and he was so drunk I don't even know if he remembers doing it. He... like, *caressed* my arm at dinner and I just went off on him and stormed out."

Nikki set a mug of hot cocoa down in front of her, and Lena sat up.

"I've been driving around for the past hour or more, trying to outrun my humiliation."

Nikki let out a sympathetic groan, and Anna rubbed Lena's back as she took a sip of hot cocoa.

"Has he texted you?" Nikki asked.

"He called twice," Lena said miserably. "I didn't pick up."

"You should talk to him," Anna counseled.

"When you're ready," Nikki added. The front door opened and she quipped, "More zombies?"

"Nope." They turned to see Gayle walking towards the kitchen, shedding her coat as she came. "Just me, but I guess zombies explains why no one is answering their phones?"

"Hot cocoa?" Nikki offered.

"Sure." Gayle sat down on Lena's other side and put an arm around her. "You know the man's been sitting in that booth for the past hour, staring down at the table?"

Lena let out an anguished sound and returned her forehead to the countertop.

"How exactly is that helpful?" Nikki asked with a wince. "She already feels bad enough as it is."

"I know that, but the point is, he *cares*."

"He cares about his sister." Lena's voice was muffled against the blue marble countertop. "He's worried sick about her, and I just *left* him there. I'm the worst."

"You were honest with him," Anna said. "That's never a bad thing. Not in the long run."

"Things will look less dire tomorrow," Nikki assured her. "Before long, it'll be another anecdote that you laugh about."

"That time you lost it under the purple lights in the bar," Gayle added.

"It will never be funny," said Lena into the marble.

Anna continued rubbing her back in circles. As she did so, she realized that this was exactly what Cee-cee had done for her when she had felt crippled by a broken heart... more than once. None of Anna's young romances had survived her constant traveling. Most men she'd left without a backward glance, but some partings had hurt more than others. The weird part was that she'd initiated this contact with Lena. A staunch "not a hugger" in most situations, physical touch was always reserved for those she cared about most—and even then, she sometimes felt awkward.

But this, right now, felt right.

"And what's going on with you?" Nikki asked. Anna looked up in surprise, but her attention was on Gayle.

"It's clearly not a good time," Gayle muttered with a glance at Lena's curls. Lena lifted her head from the countertop and looked at her big sister.

"Oh, no. Don't do that. Spill it," Lena demanded.

Gayle gave her a wry smile that didn't reach her eyes. The smile faltered and fell.

"I-I left Rex."

"Excellent," Lena said, and slumped back to the counter, chin resting on her folded arms.

Gayle looked down at her hands, twisting her wedding band around and around. "More accurately, I told him to move out. I finally confronted him about his affair." Gayle ducked her head, as if *his* betrayal was something for *her* to feel ashamed about.

"How do you feel?" Anna asked.

"Scared. I feel scared," Gayle said softly, without looking at her. "The man is useless, but he's always there. Like a piece of furniture you don't really like, but keep using anyway because it's easier than renting a truck to haul it away or buy new. I still haven't told the kids."

"Kids are resilient," Anna said. "They'll be okay."

"Plus, they're not even kids," Nikki reminded them. "They're both married. They live out of state, with busy careers and their own lives. Once they realize how much better off you are apart, they'll be happy for you."

"What will the holidays be like?" Gayle asked brokenly.

"You got the house, the booze, and the chef in this split," Anna reminded her. "I think he's the one who should worry."

"Holidays will be different," Nikki added, "and that's okay."

"Not even that different," Lena muttered. "The kids split holidays between you and the in-laws anyway."

"And you can go visit them more," Nikki told her. "Didn't they invite you last year, and Rex wouldn't take the time off work?"

Lena turned and smiled at Gayle. "You did take them on vacations without him the whole time they were teenagers. You can do that now, too."

"Even going home to that empty house feels weird. It has, ever since the kids left... but at least there was always Rex. Now it's just eerie."

"So don't go home tonight," Anna said with a shrug. "Give yourself some time."

"Are you thinking what I'm thinking?" Nikki grinned, looking from one sister to another. "Slumber party!"

"You're ridiculous," Lena muttered.

"And *you* are exceptionally morose today," Nikki said primly, "but I love you anyway."

"It's fine, I can stay at the house. I'll just put on some white noise and—"

"Stay here with us," Nikki urged. "Please. I have extra PJs and we just started a really awesome zombie movie. We can restart it, and I'll make more popcorn. Come on, Gayle, don't be a parade pooper."

Gayle rolled her eyes. "It's party pooper or raining on

your parade, not both. And I'm not in the mood for either a parade or a party."

Were those tears in her eyes?

She looked away.

"Please?" Nikki wheedled. "I'll make your favorite brownies. I've got that amazing raw milk to go with them."

The glimmer of a smile flashed across Gayle's face. "Why didn't you lead with the brownies?" she asked, shooting Nikki a grateful glance. "Thanks. I really don't want to be alone tonight."

"Anna, start the popcorn," Nikki ordered. "Gayle and Lena, come put on something comfy so we can see how this whole brain-eating thing works out."

"Speaking of Rex, I've often thought he'd be the only one safe in the event of a zombie apocalypse because he's got nothing to offer them," Lena was saying. "You might want to stay on good terms with him, just to cover your bases."

They filed out of the room, leaving Anna alone in the kitchen, smiling.

She was sorry that Lena and Gayle were in bad spots right now, but she was so grateful to be here with them.

And *for* them.

Who would've thought?

23

LENA

The slumber party idea had seemed so silly, but Lena had to admit that waking up next to a snoring Gayle had sure as heck beat waking up alone to the memory of what had happened last night with Owen.

She shot her sister one last look and closed the bedroom door behind her before peeking in on Anna and Nikki. They were both still sound asleep.

So things had gone bad with her best friend? At least she had these three to lean on. It could've been a whole lot worse...

Pinning that thought to the forefront of her mind, she padded out of the house and rushed to her car.

It was freezing outside, but she still loved this time of day. The gray morning sky tinted with the blush of the rising sun, frost dappling every surface. The air was so crisp and fresh with the promise of a new day. Lena leaned forward as she started the car, admiring the silhouettes of the bare trees against the changing colors of the sunrise. How amazing it must be to master a camera, to be able to capture moments like this and preserve them forever.

She made a mental note to ask Anna if she would show her some photography basics. It would really help if she could take some snaps on her own going forward. If the website was going to be a success, she would need to learn how to capture professional-looking shots.

She didn't bother heating the car up; she just held her breath and shivered as she drove the short distance from Nikki's house to her own. Maybe when she got there, she'd climb right back into bed and sleep the day away so she wouldn't have to think...

She spared a glance at her purse on the seat beside her and then reached for it with a groan. Her phone had died sometime after Zombie Hunter Three, and she had been too afraid to check it before that, so she had no idea if Owen had tried to call again. Part of her was glad she didn't know, but the other part really needed to hear what he had to say. Whatever it was, good or bad, at least they could begin the process of getting past it.

She hoped.

Her fingers closed over her cell and she tugged it out to plug into the car charger.

By the time it finally blinked to life, she was turning down her street. It beeped 3...4...5, geez, twelve times with saved-up notifications.

Owen must've really been—

Her thoughts were derailed as her house came into view and she saw his car parked in the driveway.

Crap.

Her pulse pounded as she pulled in beside it. She so

wasn't ready for this. She'd thought she'd have hours before having to confront this, but here he was.

She glanced briefly through his driver's side window but knew he wasn't in there. They'd had keys for one another's places for as long as they'd lived on their own. The poor man must have been sitting up in her living room all night, worrying himself sick. Just a few days after Gemma lost her husband in a car crash, Lena went and disappeared overnight.

Well done, Lena.

She opened the door gingerly and tiptoed in. Owen was fast asleep on the couch. She tried to close the door quietly, but Owen bolted upright as quickly as if she'd slammed it. He stared at her for a moment in shock and then crumpled in on himself.

"Oh, thank God," he murmured under his breath.

"I'm okay," Lena said miserably. "I slept at Nikki's."

"I know." Owen took a shuddering breath. "Nikki finally texted me back around 2 AM, after I'd already called the hospital and tried her and Gayle both. Luckily, Nikki got up to go to the bathroom and saw my text. I was going to head home once I knew you were okay, but I was so exhausted, I just fell asleep on the couch. I had the worst nightmares, and for a moment I forgot..." He shook his head. "I'm just glad you're home and safe."

She padded closer, her heart heavy. "I'm sorry I worried you. We were all watching movies together, my sisters and me. We all slept at Nikki's house. I should have texted."

She felt like a total heel for putting him through that less than a week after his brother-in-law died in a car accident.

She hadn't done it on purpose, but still. She should have thought. She should have picked up one of his calls, just to let him know she was safe. He'd been exhausted before this, and after a night with only a snatch of sleep on her couch — which was much too small for him to use as a bed — he looked worse than ever. She wanted to scoop him up and put him to bed.

"I was a mess last night," she explained shakily, "and by the time I was ready to talk about it without wanting to curl into a ball and die of embarrassment, my phone was dead and I figured you were already asleep."

"I don't care." Owen stood and closed the distance between them. "It doesn't matter. You're here now."

He wrapped her in his strong arms. For a moment, she let him hold her. But when he buried his face in her curls, she pulled away.

"Owen, I—"

"No. You said your piece last night," he said firmly. "Now it's my turn."

Owen relaxed his grip enough to look her in the eye, but he didn't let go.

"You said that it means something to you. All of this." He ran one hand down the side of her face, and she shivered. "You have to know that it means something to me too, love. I know that I smile and chat, but have you ever seen me touch another woman? Do you think I go around caressing waitresses or old ladies at the grocery?"

Lena shrugged. "I guess not?"

"I've been told I have an easy charm," Owen continued, "but that and what's between you and me? Two completely different things."

She stared up at him, scarcely believing her ears. "So you've been hitting on me on purpose?" she asked.

"Of course I was. And, frankly, it was a blow to my ego when you didn't realize," Owen chuckled. "Then, after that night when I kissed you, I worried that you *had* realized, and you were just ignoring it. Trying to let me down easy. But the way you looked at me..." He let out a groan. "Lena, you're the woman of my dreams. Quite literally. You torture me in my sleep, and then I have to see you the next day and I'm supposed to treat you like a sister? Brutal. You're gorgeous and brilliant and funny—"

"Why now?" she interrupted, overwhelmed by this outpouring of emotion but still in shock.

Owen's expression turned serious as he took a step back and rested on the arm of her couch with a weary sigh. "How could I try to be with you when I'd screwed up every single relationship I'd ever had? I thought about it, love. So many nights, I thought about telling you how I felt... but every time, I stopped myself. You mean too much to me, Lena. I couldn't risk losing you entirely. The thought of life without you if I blew it was inconceivable. I'd prefer the exquisite torture of your friendship to not having you in my life at all."

"And now?" she croaked, tears nearly choking her.

"Well, it occurred to me... what if I'm not bad at relationships? What if I was just sabotaging all of them because I wasn't with the right girl for me? I'm crazy about you, Lena." He paused, looking down at his hands, and then straightened up and looked her in the eye. "And I want us to be together. I can't promise it will be perfect. In fact," he said with a grin, "you know me too well to believe that it could be. But I can promise that I'll spend the rest of my life loving you, just as I have the first half, if you give me a chance." His face was a mask of longing. "Will you? Will you give me a chance, Lena?"

Breathless, she leaned closer and took his face in her hands.

"Yes. Of course, yes!"

Several days of stubble felt soft beneath her fingers, and for a moment, she lost herself in the warmth of his skin, the blue of those familiar eyes. She kissed him, and it felt like coming home after she had been away for far too long. Familiar and exhilarating at the same time. He pulled her into his lap, and it was a minute before she remembered what she had intended to say.

"Also, I love you, too!" There was so much more that she wanted to say to him, but for now, that was enough. It was a declaration and a promise. When she looked at him, she could see every Owen that she'd known, and even a glimpse of the man to come.

She saw the Irish boy who carried her books home in seventh grade.

The lanky teenager who would knick his dad's keys and drive them to see the sunset.

The man who showed up for her time and again, whenever she needed him.

The man she would build a life with.

Owen.

24

JACK

One week later...

Jack Merrill sat at the bar and drained the last of his beer, glancing outside at the whipping snow. The temperature had dropped a good thirty degrees over the past few days to hover around zero, and it was officially winter in Maine. Despite that, and a brutal head cold brewing, he felt better than he had in weeks.

Anna Sullivan was finally gone, and she'd taken all the drama and strife alone with her.

"Want another or you done?"

He looked up at his twin sister and shook his head. "Just the one. It's not coming down hard enough to accumulate much, but it's definitely going to get slippery out there."

Everyone knew that black ice was much harder to navigate than snow.

Gayle took his empty glass and set a bowl of house-made

spiced nuts in front of him. He let out a grunt of thanks as he dug in.

"You missed a really fun party last night, you know," she said, swiping at some nearby crumbs with a hand towel.

He'd been invited—more than once, by all three of his sisters—to what they'd not-so cleverly dubbed the "Merrill Early Family Christmas", and he'd declined each time, without elaborating. They knew his reasons. Apparently Gayle hadn't gotten the message yet.

"Yeah, I really wish I could've been there...wait, no I don't," he deadpanned with a scowl. "And I wish you'd stop talking to me about it, Gayle."

She looked away at his use of her given name. Usually, when he was talking directly to her, he called her "Gee".

Unless he was mad.

Really mad.

Despite his obvious anger, she had no qualms about snapping back at him.

"Yeah? Well, so long as we're sharing our wish lists, I wish you'd stop being so freaking bullheaded." She waved the towel in the air. "I know, I know, you're Jack Merrill. A loner. A maverick. An army of one, with marching orders to shut down when anyone tries to press you on anything, but this is getting silly. Are you really just going to go MIA every time Anna comes to town?"

Seemed about right to him. Given the fact that he'd already forgiven both Lena and Nikki after they ambushed him at this very bar not three weeks back, he thought he'd been pretty compromising. But leave it to Gayle to push for a mile when he gave her inches.

"Yup. That's the idea," he muttered, glancing up at the

clock over the bar. He'd planned to stay another half hour and have a meal, but he wasn't loving the current ambience. He shoved back his stool and moved to stand as Gayle closed the distance between them, leaning over the bar.

"It's not healthy, Jack," she murmured, her tone low and concerned. "Throwing up these walls every time something hurts you. You're not too old to change, you know."

His sister had stayed married to that clown for more than half her life. Now she finally worked up the nerve to dump him, and suddenly she was Confucius?

"That's the thing you don't get. I don't want to change, Gayle."

He stood and reached into his jeans pocket to pull out a twenty.

"Now, if you'll excuse me, I'm going to go home, heat up a can of soup, and eat it without being harassed."

Why was it so hard to get a little peace around here lately?

Gayle opened her mouth to jaw back at him, but then stopped short as her cheeks went ashy.

He frowned and stared at her.

"What's the matter?" he demanded. "Did you just see a ghost or something?"

She wet her lips, eyes glued to a spot behind him.

"Not exactly...but pretty close."

He turned and followed her gaze to a woman standing just a few feet away. Her head was turned, so he could only see her profile, but something about her was so familiar. Snow-kissed, honey-blonde hair piled on top of her head in a loose knot, a pert nose that led to full lips...

Just then, as if she felt his gaze, she turned to face him full on.

The breath left him in a whoosh as a blast from the past hit him straight in the solar plexus.

Corinne.

Aside from the unanswered texts she sent him every year on August 8th, he hadn't seen or heard from her in nearly twenty years.

Not since right after—

"Hello, Jack."

Blood pounded in his ears as he turned back toward the bar and gestured for Gayle to get him another drink. She could drive him home.

His mind reeled as he tried to make sense of all this. What the hell was Corinne doing in Cherry Blossom Point? The last he'd heard, she was married with a kid, living in Schenectady or something.

But as she sidled up and took the empty seat beside him, he knew he already had his answer.

This was no crazy coincidence, and she hadn't come to see his sister for some long-delayed coffee talk.

She was here for him.

"Gayle," Corinne said, nodding to his sister.

Gayle set the beer down and smiled. "Hey, Corinne. How've you been?"

Corinne wriggled out of her coat and shrugged. "Not bad."

"What can I get you?"

A taxi? he wanted to add.

"Just a cup of coffee, if you have it."

God, even her voice hurt to listen to.

It wasn't that he hated her—in fact, that was the furthest thing from the truth—but not only was she a brutal reminder of everything he'd had and lost, seeing her face just drove the ever-present spike of guilt deeper into his heart.

He'd failed her. He'd failed their son, and nothing would ever change that.

She leaned closer and down into his line of sight, bringing a waft of honeysuckle perfume with her.

"How have you been, Jack?"

He met her gaze and then wished he didn't. Now that the shock had worn off, he'd hoped he'd been wrong after that first glance. Hoped that maybe he'd hardly even recognize her, but she looked the same as ever. Maybe more beautiful, if that was possible. More mature, for certain. Her cheeks were a little leaner, her eyes wiser...

"You came all the way here from wherever the hell you live now to ask me how I'm doing, Corinne?"

For a long moment, she was silent, and then she shook her head. "Even I'm not that much of a masochist, Jack. No, I came here to ask a favor..."

Did you like Lena and Owen's story? Stay tuned for Just Getting Started, Jack's story, out now and FREE in KU!

When Jack Merrill's ex comes to ask him a personal favor, he wants to say no. Having her back in Cherry Blossom Point is nothing but a crushing reminder of the son they lost so tragically two decades before. Still, when he finds out that the safety of her daughter is at stake, he can't refuse...But that doesn't mean he has to like it.

Corinne Michaels' life comes full circle when circumstances force her to confront the past. She and Jack were far too immature to have a child back then, but she never regretted it...not even when they lost him. Grief, time, and distance have kept them apart for nearly twenty year, but when her daughter's life is threatened, there is only one person Corinne trusts enough to help protect her.

Gayle Merrill has finally worked up the courage to pull the plug on her deeply broken marriage. As much as she'd hoped her life would get better the second Rex was out the door, she realizes very quickly that she has some deep soul-searching to do.

It wasn't the hooting of the great-horned owl that woke him. Not the katydids or the crickets, or even the bullfrogs. In fact, Jack always slept better when the sounds of nature surrounded him.

It was the strange sensation of sleeping so deeply, he could no longer hear them, that had him forcing his heavy lids open.

Jack was usually a light sleeper. He'd become hyper-aware of his surroundings during his years in the Marines, and countless nights of camping in the wilderness had done nothing to change that. There were bears in these woods, and he was never one to be caught off guard.

When his son was a baby, Jack had woken at the first sound of fussing. Even eight years later, he still slept lightly. He always looked in on his son at dawn, just to hear the steady sound of his breathing and take in his sweet sleeping face before he started his day.

Using all his strength, he rolled over and flicked on his bedside light, wincing as pain shot through his head. He looked around, dazed and disoriented by his surroundings.

A tiny room with a metal bed frame and rough wooden walls.

The cabin.

They were in a tiny cabin on the shore of Jack's favorite lake, tucked away in the mountains. Jack and River had arrived two days ago for their annual fishing trip. They had gone as a family when River was only a few months old, and had kept coming every year, even after Jack and Corinne split up. It had become an annual father and son trip, something that they both looked forward to all year long.

"It's better than Christmas, Dad!" River had told him two days before as he'd climbed into Jack's truck.

River.

The thought of him had Jack trying to roll out of bed, but his arms and legs were as heavy as lead, stuck fast to the bed. It was like he was lying in a pool of molasses. His throat was so dry that he could hardly swallow, and his mouth felt like it was full of cotton. He forced his eyes open in the darkness, trying to recall the night before. Did he drink? No, of course not. He never drank when River was with him.

A sudden cramp seized his stomach. The flu? Doubtful. It wasn't even flu season yet, and he rarely got sick. Had they eaten something bad? Unlikely. They'd had fresh trout for dinner, one that River had reeled in all by himself. Just fish and some roasted potatoes. A wave of nausea rolled through him. Not their dinner, then, but something. The water?

Whatever the case, if he felt this bad, a much smaller River must feel even worse.

That boy was his whole life...Where was he?

Just down the hall. The room with a view of the lake, he always claimed it.

Jack willed his legs to move. He stood and lurched towards the door, leaning against the rough cabin walls as he moved down the dark hallway. His head spun — the whole hallway seemed to spin — and the journey felt like miles instead of just a few feet. When he finally reached the open doorway of his son's room, the sounds of the night almost seemed to stop as he listened for the steady rhythm of River's breathing...

Why couldn't he hear River breathing?

Jack stumbled to the bed, almost landing on top of his motionless son. His heart stuttered as he took River's face in his hands. His skin was cold, so very cold...

"No!"

Jack awoke with a hoarse cry, heart hammering in his chest, body slick with a cold sweat. It took a few minutes for the panic and fear to subside, longer for Jack to come fully into the present and glance at his bedside clock.

5:40 AM.

Damn. It had been a long, brutal night.

There were some dreams that Jack wanted to live in. Nights that he dreamed of River when he was still alive, of their adventures climbing mountains or digging huge holes at the beach...nights when he revisited all of the most joyful moments of fatherhood. Teaching River how to swim, how to ride a bike. There were mornings when Jack didn't want to wake up.

And then there were mornings like this one... mornings

that he was desperate to get out of bed, desperate to think about anything else... or about nothing at all. Long ago, he'd turned to drink. These days, he exercised instead.

It took another ten minutes for his legs to stop quaking enough for him to stand, dress, and make his way downstairs.

Classic rock blasted through his headphones, drowning out his thoughts as he put every piece of equipment in his home gym through its paces. He didn't stop until his muscles were screaming — and for Jack, that took some doing. He might have hit the half-century mark, but he was in better shape than most men twenty years younger. It wasn't a point of pride or vanity. It was a condition born of necessity. Without the gym...without hiking and rowing in the great outdoors, he wouldn't have a moment of peace.

Still breathing hard, he shut off his music and began wiping everything down. It had been weeks since he'd dreamed of that terrible night. Long enough to give him a tiny shred of hope that it'd been the last time. But he, of all people, knew what a terrible joke hope was.

He had clung to a shred of hope on that awful night twenty years before. He'd known that River was gone before he'd even touched his icy face, and yet he'd hoped...

Once his poison-addled brain had realized that the cabin was full of carbon monoxide, he'd carried River out of the house and laid him on the lawn. Jack had breathed into his mouth, pounded on his chest... and nothing. He'd left his boy long enough to run back inside and phone an ambulance, then gone back out and continued his futile efforts. He'd lost all sense of time, but judging by how long it took an ambulance to get out to the cabin, he was probably working for thirty senseless minutes to bring River back. By the time the ambulance reached him, he'd been half-dead from a combination of poison and exhaustion himself.

And even then, some shard of hope had remained stuck in his chest... hope that the medic would find a pulse, some sign of life that Jack was too affected by the gas to feel. He sat there cradling his dead son in his arms, bargaining away everything he had for one more chance. A rewind. A single do-over. He'd still possessed a shred of faith that night too, because he'd spoken directly to God. Hell, he'd begged.

Take me. Take me instead.

Fat lot of good that had done.

Forget hope. Forget faith. Fickle flirts, the both of them.

Jack toweled the sweat off of his body and pulled his t-shirt back on before walking upstairs. He yanked open a cabinet door and grabbed a bag of instant coffee. He mixed it with some scalding-hot water and drank it black as he watched the world wake up. The windows of his house looked out into the woods, and there were always birds at the edge of his yard, always birdsong. Birds were good. They kept the silence at bay.

He turned away and used the last of the hot water to mix a bowl of plain rolled oats as his mind began to hum. There was no question of why the dream had come back today. He'd have to see *her* again. Her golden eyes, the exact same color as their son's.

Corinne.

She had come into his sister's bar, The Milky Thistle, two weeks before. Had traveled to Cherry Blossom Point just to find Jack and ask him for a favor. He couldn't say no to Corinne. Not the day he met her, and not now. Especially not now. If it wasn't for him, their son would still be alive. Surely, if she asked a favor, it was the least he could do.

But it had been a big one.

A knock sounded at the front door. Before he could reach it, someone unlocked the door from the outside and it swung open. His twin brushed past him and walked into the kitchen carrying a white paper bag.

"Big day today, huh, little brother?" Gayle was ten minutes older than Jack, an irrelevant fact that she enjoyed reminding him of. She dumped his watery oatmeal down the drain.

"I wasn't done with that," Jack grumbled.

"No one should eat that on purpose." Gayle pulled a bundle of aluminum foil from her bag and tossed it at him. It was warm and smelled like smoked meat. He sat at the counter and unwrapped the package to find a croissant stuffed with bacon, egg, and cheese. A glance confirmed that the bag had *Sadie's* printed on the back of it. His ex-wife made a mean croissant, and his stomach was growling after his workout, so he took a bite.

He had to admit, the sandwich was a lot better than the plain oats and four raw eggs he normally consumed after he exercised.

Gayle whisked Jack's coffee away, and it followed the oatmeal down the drain. She set to work brewing a "proper" pot in the percolator, as if it made any difference.

"What are you doing here, Gayle? It's not even 8 o'clock." He was usually up before the sun, but Gayle was a professional night owl. Her bar, The Milky Thistle, kept her out past midnight more often than not.

"I was up early," Gayle said, staring into his empty

refrigerator as if she expected cream to appear out of thin air. "The house felt so big and empty, and I didn't want to eat breakfast alone."

Ever since Gayle had tossed her philandering husband to the curb, she had been a lot more open about her feelings. Jack respected her honesty; he hated a fake smile. But did she have to talk about them *so* much? Maybe it was good for her, all this unloading. It was her prerogative and he was happy to roll with it... as long as she didn't expect the same from him.

"Close the fridge," Jack ordered. "There's a can of milk in the cupboard if you won't drink it black."

Gayle shot him a look and closed the door of the fridge harder than she needed to. She poured two fresh cups of coffee and sat down to unwrap her breakfast sandwich.

"How's it going with Rex, anyway?" he asked. "Are you divorced yet?"

"Ha, no. As you well know, it takes a lot longer than just a couple weeks. And that's when you get along with your ex. So far, it's not going great." Gayle ate a bite of her sandwich and then continued, "I make quite a lot more than he does, did you know that? He was always job-hopping and then that long, 'lay around the house and play video games era'...I should have left him before the bar turned a profit. Now, he wants a percentage of the business, along with the house and alimony."

A bolt of anger shot through him. "What a worm."

"He's worse. Even worms produce something of value." Gayle sighed and hung her head. "I shouldn't say that. We have two beautiful children. He gave me that. I just can't believe his demands, after he..." She shook her head and returned her attention to her breakfast.

His twin didn't need to elaborate. They didn't talk about it much, but Rex had been a crappy husband. He had cheated on her repeatedly, not even bothering to hide with his recent mistress. To demand the family home and a share of the business that Gayle had built herself, with zero help from him...

Anger simmered in the marrow of Jack's bones.

"It would be easier if he just disappeared," he said quietly. He glanced at Gayle and she met his gaze with a smirk as he raised his eyebrows in a question.

I can make that happen if you want me to.

Gayle looked away with a crack of laughter. "You can take the man out of the Marines, but you'll never take the Marines out of the man." She took a sip of her coffee and grimaced.

Jack shook his head and took another bite of food. As if the Marines had anything to do with anything. That was a lifetime ago. He'd joined up as a kid and left the military when River was born. No, wanting to kill Rex was just a normal response to seeing his sister treated like garbage for years. He'd fantasized about it, more than once... but he didn't have it in him to kill someone who didn't pose an active threat, no matter what a garbage human being they were. Anyway, he loved his niece and nephew too much to do that to their dad.

Unless, of course, Gayle really wanted him to...

He glanced at her again.

"Stop it. I do not want you to kill Rex and hide his body in the woods," she said primly, "but I appreciate the offer."

Jack shrugged. "Roger that. So what's the plan, then?"

"My lawyer is working on it. We'll have to see. But I came

here to check on *you*. I wanted to see how you were feeling about today."

"It's just another job."

Gayle snorted. "Liar. Come on, Jack, it's me. We shared a crowded apartment filled with amniotic fluid for nine of our most formative months. Be real with me."

"I hate it when you mention amniotic fluid when I'm eating."

"As if what you were eating was any less gross." She rolled her eyes and then stared at him, waiting.

"Okay, you want the truth? I'm not looking forward to it," he admitted at last. "Corinne is in the past. She should have stayed there."

Corinne had an eighteen-year-old daughter named Kiera. She'd gone to her college orientation weekend a few months before. On the second night, she was assaulted on the way back from a party. Three drunken frat boys had pulled her into the bushes, and she had been rescued by campus police moments before the unthinkable happened. Corinne's daughter had returned home traumatized and terrified. She'd been withdrawn and listless ever since. No interest in returning to college, no interest in anything at all... She had hardly emerged from her room. Mother and daughter had both gone to therapy, and apparently, the shrink had suggested self-defense classes. The idea was to boost the kid's confidence so that she could start back at college in the spring.

Jack had almost said no. He'd wanted to. But how could he?

His school was the best in New England. And no one would work harder than he would.

Gayle sighed and cupped her mug. "You *put* Corinne in the past, Jack. She tried to stay in touch. She still texts you every year on Riv's birthday. You never even reply. Frankly, I'm amazed she even wanted to see you."

"Same here."

Who wanted to see the person responsible for the death of their son?

"That's not what I meant!" Gayle grabbed his face and turned it towards her. Her hand was shaking. "It wasn't your fault, Jack! No one thought that, not ever. No one but you."

No one else was there. No one but him and River.

Had he died in his sleep? Or had he woken up, first, too sick to get out of bed, waiting for him to come and make it better? He could have called out while Jack was too deeply asleep to hear him. That was what Jack believed, in his lowest moments. His son had died alone and afraid, all because his father had failed to protect him.

The thought gutted him, every time.

"Fine. You want to clam up like always, I can't stop you." Gayle sighed and stood, taking their mugs to the sink. With her back to him, she said, "At least I got a proper meal and some real coffee into you before your big day."

Big day, he scoffed internally. Jack had been entirely unable to protect their son from dying, incapable of protecting his baby sister Nikki from being abused and nearly killed by her ex-husband... and still, for some reason he couldn't fathom, Corinne thought that *he* was the best choice to ensure her daughter's safety.

It felt like a cruel joke.

River would be a grown man now, if it wasn't for Jack's carelessness.

But he had already failed Corinne once. He had failed their son. How could he refuse her anything? There was no choice for him, not really. He would do everything he could to protect Corinne's daughter, to help both of them feel safe.

And even though he knew that he didn't deserve it, even though he knew that he would never *get* it... a tiny part of him couldn't help but wonder if he might find even a breath of redemption in the process.

Get the rest of Just Getting Started, Jack's story, out now and FREE in KU!

ALSO BY CHRISTINE GAEL

Want to get an alert next time a new book is out, find out about sales or contests, and chat with Christine? Join the mailing list **here!**

Maeve's Girls

(Standalone Women's Fiction)

Bluebird Bay

Finding Tomorrow

Finding Home

Finding Peace

Finding Forever

Finding Forgiveness

Finding Acceptance

Finding Redemption

Finding Refuge

Cherry Blossom Point

Starting From Scratch

Just Getting Started

A Fresh Start

Lucky Strickland Series (Mystery/Thriller)

Lucky Break

Getting Lucky

Crow's Feet Coven (Paranormal Women's Fiction)

Writing Wrongs

Brewing Trouble

Stealing Time

Made in the USA
Monee, IL
18 September 2022

14185232R00152